JULIUS CAESAR

WILLIAM SHAKESPEARE

FP CLASSICS

Published 2025

FiNGERPRINT! CLASSICS
Prakash Books

Fingerprint Publishing
@FingerprintP
@fingerprintpublishingbooks
www.fingerprintpublishing.com

ISBN: 978 93 8653 804 8

William Shakespeare began his career as an actor, writer, and part owner of a playing company called the Lord Chamberlain's Men, later known as King's Men, in London. Often regarded as the 'Bard of Avon' he is one of the world's pre-eminent dramatists. Born and brought up in Stratford-upon-Avon, he married Anne Hathaway at the age of eighteen and they had three children—Susanna, and twins Hamnet and Judith. Though few records survive of his private life, he appeared to have retired to Stratford around 1613 where he died three years later.

His works still in existence, including some collaborations, consist of thirty-eight plays, one hundred and fifty-four sonnets, two long narrative poems, and several other verses. His plays are performed much more than any other playwright's and have been translated in almost all major languages. Most of his known works have been produced between 1589 and 1613. His early plays were mainly comedies and histories which remain regarded as some of the best works produced in these genres.

Shakespeare's plays are difficult to date. His early classical and Italianate comedies contain tight double plots and precise comic sequences giving way to the romantic atmosphere of his most acclaimed comedies in the mid-1590s. *A Midsummer Night's Dream*—a witty mixture of romance, fairy magic, and comic low life scenes—is one of his most delightful creations shortly before he turned to *Romeo and Juliet. Romeo and Juliet* is his most famous romantic tragedy of sexually charged adolescence, love, and death. It marks a departure from his earlier works and from others of the English Renaissance.

His plays demonstrate the expansiveness of his imagination and the extent of his learning. Shakespeare's sequence of great comedies continues with *Merchant of Venice, Much Ado About Nothing*, *As You Like It*, and *Twelfth Night.* One of his best-loved comedies, *Twelfth Night* is a romantic drama of confusions, comic sequences, and mistaken identities.

Shakespeare introduced prose comedy in the histories of the late 1590s—*Henry IV, Part I* and *Part II, and Henry V*—after the lyrical *Richard II. Julius Caesar* introduced a new kind of drama. Based on true events from Roman history, this tale of assassination of Julius Caesar, the powerful Roman politician, is one of Shakespeare's most loved political tragedies.

Shakespeare wrote the so-called 'problem plays' in the early 17th century. *Measure for Measure*, *Troilus and Cressida*, and *All's Well that Ends Well* being a few of them. Until about 1608, he mainly wrote tragedies including *Hamlet*, *Othello*, *King Lear*, and *Macbeth.* The story of a brave Scottish general named Macbeth, the eponymous drama illustrates how the lust for power dooms the fate of a noble person.

Antony and Cleopatra and *Coriolanus*—his last major tragedies, contain some of his finest poetry. Shakespeare wrote tragicomedies, also known as romances, in his last phase. These include *Cymbeline*, *The Winter's Tale*, and *The Tempest*, as well as the collaboration *Pericles, Prince of Tyre.*

A true genius, Shakespeare's popular characters and plots are studied, performed, reinterpreted, and discussed till today. William Shakespeare, known as the English national poet, is considered the greatest dramatist of all time.

Contents

CHARACTERS OF THE PLAY

JULIUS CAESAR, Roman statesman and general.

OCTAVIUS, Triumvir after Caesar's death, later Augustus Caesar, first emperor of Rome.

MARK ANTONY, general and friend of Caesar, a Triumvir after his death.

LEPIDUS, third member of the Triumvirate.

MARCUS BRUTUS, leader of the conspiracy against Caesar.

CASSIUS, instigator of the conspiracy.

CASCA TREBONIUS LIGARIUS DECIUS BRUTUS METELLUS CIMBER CINNA	conspirators against Caesar.

CALPURNIA, wife of Caesar.

PORTIA, wife of Brutus.

CICERO POPILIUS PUBLIUS	senators.

FLAVIUS and MARULLUS, tribunes.

CATO LUCILIUS TITINIUS MESSALA VOLUMNIUS	supportors of Brutus.

ARTEMIDORUS, a teacher of rhetoric.

CINNA THE POET.

Varro Clitus Claudius Strato Lucius Dardanius	servants to Brutus.

Pindarus, servant to Cassius.

The Ghost of Caesar.

A Soothsayer.

A Poet.

Senators, Citizens, Soldiers, Commoners, Messengers, and Servants

Scene:
Rome, the conspirators' camp near Sardis, and the plains of Philippi.

Act 1

Scene I. Rome. A Street.

Enter FLAVIUS, MARULLUS, and certain Commoners

FLAVIUS

Hence! home, you idle creatures get you home.
Is this a holiday? What! know you not,
Being mechanical, you ought not walk
Upon a labouring day without the sign
Of your profession? Speak, what trade art thou?

FIRST COMMONER

Why, sir, a carpenter.

MARULLUS

Where is thy leather apron and thy rule?
What dost thou with thy best apparel on?
You, sir, what trade are you?

SECOND COMMONER

Truly, sir, in respect of a fine workman, I am but, as you would say, a cobbler.

MARULLUS

But what trade art thou? Answer me directly.

SECOND COMMONER

A trade, sir, that, I hope, I may use with a safe conscience; which is, indeed, sir, a mender of bad soles.

MARULLUS

What trade, thou knave? Thou naughty knave, what trade?

SECOND COMMONER

Nay, I beseech you, sir, be not out with me; yet, if you be out, sir, I can mend you.

MARULLUS

What meanest thou by that? Mend me, thou saucy fellow!

SECOND COMMONER

Why, sir, cobble you.

FLAVIUS

Thou art a cobbler, art thou?

SECOND COMMONER

Truly, sir, all that I live by is with the awl: I meddle with no tradesman's matters, nor women's matters, but with awl. I am, indeed, sir, a surgeon to old shoes; when they are in great danger, I recover them.

As proper men as ever trod upon neat's leather have gone upon my handiwork.

FLAVIUS

But wherefore art not in thy shop to-day?
Why dost thou lead these men about the streets?

SECOND COMMONER

Truly, sir, to wear out their shoes, to get myself into more work. But, indeed, sir, we make holiday, to see Caesar and to rejoice in his triumph.

MARULLUS

Wherefore rejoice? What conquest brings he home?
What tributaries follow him to Rome,
To grace in captive bonds his chariot-wheels?
You blocks, you stones, you worse than senseless things!
O you hard hearts, you cruel men of Rome,
Knew you not Pompey? Many a time and oft
Have you climb'd up to walls and battlements,
To towers and windows, yea, to chimney-tops,
Your infants in your arms, and there have sat
The livelong day, with patient expectation,
To see great Pompey pass the streets of Rome:
And when you saw his chariot but appear,

Have you not made an universal shout,
That Tiber trembled underneath her banks,
To hear the replication of your sounds
Made in her concave shores?
And do you now put on your best attire?
And do you now cull out a holiday?
And do you now strew flowers in his way
That comes in triumph over Pompey's blood? Be gone!
Run to your houses, fall upon your knees,
Pray to the gods to intermit the plague
That needs must light on this ingratitude.

FLAVIUS

Go, go, good countrymen, and, for this fault,
Assemble all the poor men of your sort;
Draw them to Tiber banks, and weep your tears
Into the channel, till the lowest stream
Do kiss the most exalted shores of all.

Exeunt all the Commoners

See whether their basest metal be not moved;
They vanish tongue-tied in their guiltiness.
Go you down that way towards the Capitol;
This way will I. Disrobe the images,
If you do find them deck'd with ceremonies.

MARULLUS

May we do so?

You know it is the feast of Lupercal.

FLAVIUS

It is no matter; let no images
Be hung with Caesar's trophies. I'll about,
And drive away the vulgar from the streets:
So do you too, where you perceive them thick.
These growing feathers pluck'd from Caesar's wing
Will make him fly an ordinary pitch,
Who else would soar above the view of men
And keep us all in servile fearfulness.

Exeunt

Scene II. A Public Place.

Flourish. Enter CAESAR; ANTONY, for the course; CALPURNIA, PORTIA, DECIUS BRUTUS, CICERO, BRUTUS, CASSIUS, and CASCA; a great crowd following, among them a Soothsayer

CAESAR

Calpurnia!

CASCA

Peace, ho! Caesar speaks.

CAESAR

Calpurnia!

CALPURNIA

Here, my lord.

CAESAR

Stand you directly in Antonius' way,
When he doth run his course. Antonius!

ANTONY

Caesar, my lord?

CAESAR

Forget not, in your speed, Antonius,
To touch Calpurnia; for our elders say,
The barren, touched in this holy chase,
Shake off their sterile curse.

ANTONY

I shall remember:
When Caesar says 'do this,' it is perform'd.

CAESAR

Set on; and leave no ceremony out.

Flourish

SOOTHSAYER

Caesar!

CAESAR

Ha! Who calls?

CASCA

Bid every noise be still: peace yet again!

CAESAR

Who is it in the press that calls on me?
I hear a tongue, shriller than all the music,
Cry 'Caesar!' Speak; Caesar is turn'd to hear.

SOOTHSAYER

Beware the ides of March.

CAESAR

What man is that?

BRUTUS

A soothsayer bids you beware the ides of March.

CAESAR

Set him before me; let me see his face.

CASSIUS

Fellow, come from the throng; look upon Caesar.

CAESAR

What say'st thou to me now? Speak once again.

SOOTHSAYER

Beware the ides of March.

CAESAR

He is a dreamer; let us leave him: pass.

Sennet. Exeunt all except
BRUTUS and CASSIUS

CASSIUS

Will you go see the order of the course?

BRUTUS

Not I.

CASSIUS

I pray you, do.

BRUTUS

I am not gamesome: I do lack some part
Of that quick spirit that is in Antony.
Let me not hinder, Cassius, your desires;
I'll leave you.

CASSIUS

Brutus, I do observe you now of late:
I have not from your eyes that gentleness
And show of love as I was wont to have:
You bear too stubborn and too strange a hand
Over your friend that loves you.

BRUTUS

Cassius,
Be not deceived: if I have veil'd my look,
I turn the trouble of my countenance
Merely upon myself. Vexed I am
Of late with passions of some difference,
Conceptions only proper to myself,

Which give some soil perhaps to my behaviors;
But let not therefore my good friends be grieved—
Among which number, Cassius, be you one—
Nor construe any further my neglect,
Than that poor Brutus, with himself at war,
Forgets the shows of love to other men.

CASSIUS

Then, Brutus, I have much mistook your passion;
By means whereof this breast of mine hath buried
Thoughts of great value, worthy cogitations.
Tell me, good Brutus, can you see your face?

BRUTUS

No, Cassius; for the eye sees not itself,
But by reflection, by some other things.

CASSIUS

'Tis just;
And it is very much lamented, Brutus,
That you have no such mirrors as will turn
Your hidden worthiness into your eye,
That you might see your shadow. I have heard,
Where many of the best respect in Rome,
Except immortal Caesar, speaking of Brutus
And groaning underneath this age's yoke,
Have wish'd that noble Brutus had his eyes.

BRUTUS

Into what dangers would you lead me, Cassius,
That you would have me seek into myself
For that which is not in me?

CASSIUS

Therefore, good Brutus, be prepared to hear;
And since you know you cannot see yourself
So well as by reflection, I, your glass,
Will modestly discover to yourself
That of yourself which you yet know not of.
And be not jealous on me, gentle Brutus:
Were I a common laugher, or did use
To stale with ordinary oaths my love
To every new protester; if you know
That I do fawn on men and hug them hard
And after scandal them, or if you know
That I profess myself in banqueting
To all the rout, then hold me dangerous.

Flourish, and shout

BRUTUS

What means this shouting? I do fear, the people
Choose Caesar for their king.

CASSIUS

Ay, do you fear it?

Then must I think you would not have it so.

BRUTUS

I would not, Cassius; yet I love him well.
But wherefore do you hold me here so long?
What is it that you would impart to me?
If it be aught toward the general good,
Set honour in one eye and death i' the other,
And I will look on both indifferently;
For let the gods so speed me as I love
The name of honour more than I fear death.

CASSIUS

I know that virtue to be in you, Brutus,
As well as I do know your outward favour.
Well, honour is the subject of my story.
I cannot tell what you and other men
Think of this life; but, for my single self,
I had as lief not be as live to be
In awe of such a thing as I myself.
I was born free as Caesar; so were you.
We both have fed as well, and we can both
Endure the winter's cold as well as he.
For once, upon a raw and gusty day,
The troubled Tiber chafing with her shores,
Caesar said to me 'Darest thou, Cassius, now

Leap in with me into this angry flood,
And swim to yonder point?' Upon the word,
Accoutred as I was, I plunged in
And bade him follow; so indeed he did.
The torrent roar'd, and we did buffet it
With lusty sinews, throwing it aside
And stemming it with hearts of controversy;
But ere we could arrive the point proposed,
Caesar cried 'Help me, Cassius, or I sink!'
I, as Aeneas, our great ancestor,
Did from the flames of Troy upon his shoulder
The old Anchises bear, so from the waves of Tiber
Did I the tired Caesar. And this man
Is now become a god, and Cassius is
A wretched creature and must bend his body,
If Caesar carelessly but nod on him.
He had a fever when he was in Spain,
And when the fit was on him, I did mark
How he did shake. 'Tis true, this god did shake.
His coward lips did from their colour fly,
And that same eye whose bend doth awe the world
Did lose his lustre. I did hear him groan.
Ay, and that tongue of his that bade the Romans
Mark him and write his speeches in their books,

Alas, it cried 'Give me some drink, Titinius,'
As a sick girl. Ye gods, it doth amaze me
A man of such a feeble temper should
So get the start of the majestic world
And bear the palm alone.

Shout. Flourish

BRUTUS

Another general shout!
I do believe that these applauses are
For some new honours that are heap'd on Caesar.

CASSIUS

Why, man, he doth bestride the narrow world
Like a Colossus, and we petty men
Walk under his huge legs and peep about
To find ourselves dishonourable graves.
Men at some time are masters of their fates:
The fault, dear Brutus, is not in our stars,
But in ourselves, that we are underlings.
Brutus and Caesar: what should be in that 'Caesar'?
Why should that name be sounded more than yours?
Write them together, yours is as fair a name.
Sound them, it doth become the mouth as well;
Weigh them, it is as heavy; conjure with 'em,
Brutus will start a spirit as soon as Caesar.

Now, in the names of all the gods at once,
Upon what meat doth this our Caesar feed,
That he is grown so great? Age, thou art shamed!
Rome, thou hast lost the breed of noble bloods!
When went there by an age, since the great flood,
But it was famed with more than with one man?
When could they say till now, that talk'd of Rome,
That her wide walls encompass'd but one man?
Now is it Rome indeed and room enough,
When there is in it but one only man.
O, you and I have heard our fathers say,
There was a Brutus once that would have brook'd
The eternal devil to keep his state in Rome
As easily as a king.

BRUTUS

That you do love me, I am nothing jealous;
What you would work me to, I have some aim;
How I have thought of this and of these times,
I shall recount hereafter; for this present,
I would not, so with love I might entreat you,
Be any further moved. What you have said
I will consider; what you have to say
I will with patience hear, and find a time
Both meet to hear and answer such high things.

Till then, my noble friend, chew upon this:
Brutus had rather be a villager
Than to repute himself a son of Rome
Under these hard conditions as this time
Is like to lay upon us.

CASSIUS

I am glad that my weak words
Have struck but thus much show of fire from
Brutus.

BRUTUS

The games are done and Caesar is returning.

CASSIUS

As they pass by, pluck Casca by the sleeve;
And he will, after his sour fashion, tell you
What hath proceeded worthy note to-day.

Re-enter CAESAR and his Train

BRUTUS

I will do so. But, look you, Cassius,
The angry spot doth glow on Caesar's brow,
And all the rest look like a chidden train;
Calpurnia's cheek is pale; and Cicero
Looks with such ferret and such fiery eyes
As we have seen him in the Capitol,
Being cross'd in conference by some senators.

CASSIUS

Casca will tell us what the matter is.

CAESAR

Antonius!

ANTONY

Caesar?

CAESAR

Let me have men about me that are fat;
Sleek-headed men and such as sleep o' nights.
Yond Cassius has a lean and hungry look;
He thinks too much: such men are dangerous.

ANTONY

Fear him not, Caesar; he's not dangerous;
He is a noble Roman and well given.

CAESAR

Would he were fatter! But I fear him not.
Yet if my name were liable to fear,
I do not know the man I should avoid
So soon as that spare Cassius. He reads much;
He is a great observer and he looks
Quite through the deeds of men: he loves no plays,
As thou dost, Antony; he hears no music.
Seldom he smiles, and smiles in such a sort
As if he mock'd himself and scorn'd his spirit

That could be moved to smile at anything.
Such men as he be never at heart's ease
Whiles they behold a greater than themselves,
And therefore are they very dangerous.
I rather tell thee what is to be fear'd
Than what I fear; for always I am Caesar.
Come on my right hand, for this ear is deaf,
And tell me truly what thou think'st of him.

Sennet. Exeunt CAESAR and all his Train, but CASCA

CASCA

You pull'd me by the cloak; would you speak with me?

BRUTUS

Ay, Casca; tell us what hath chanced to-day,
That Caesar looks so sad?

CASCA

Why, you were with him, were you not?

BRUTUS

I should not then ask Casca what had chanced.

CASCA

Why, there was a crown offered him: and being offered him, he put it by with the back of his hand, thus; and then the people fell a-shouting.

BRUTUS

What was the second noise for?

CASCA

Why, for that too.

CASSIUS

They shouted thrice: what was the last cry for?

CASCA

Why, for that too.

BRUTUS

Was the crown offered him thrice?

CASCA

Ay, marry, was't, and he put it by thrice, every time gentler than other, and at every putting-by mine honest neighbours shouted.

CASSIUS

Who offered him the crown?

CASCA

Why, Antony.

BRUTUS

Tell us the manner of it, gentle Casca.

CASCA

I can as well be hanged as tell the manner of it: it was mere foolery; I did not mark it. I saw Mark Antony offer him a crown—yet 'twas not a crown neither, 'twas one of these coronets—and, as I told you, he put it by once; but, for all that, to my thinking, he would fain have had it. Then he offered it to him again; then he put it by again; but, to my thinking, he was very loath to lay his fingers off it. And then he offered it the third time; he put it the third time by; and still as he refused it, the rabblement hooted and clapped their chapped hands and threw up their sweaty night-caps and uttered such a deal of stinking breath because Caesar refused the crown that it had almost choked Caesar; for he swooned and fell down at it. And for mine own part, I durst not laugh, for fear of opening my lips and receiving the bad air.

CASSIUS

But, soft, I pray you: what, did Caesar swoon?

CASCA

He fell down in the market-place, and foamed at mouth, and was speechless.

BRUTUS

'Tis very like: he hath the failing sickness.

CASSIUS

No, Caesar hath it not; but you and I,
And honest Casca, we have the falling sickness.

CASCA

I know not what you mean by that; but, I am sure, Caesar fell down. If the tag-rag people did not clap him and hiss him, according as he pleased and displeased them, as they use to do the players in the theatre, I am no true man.

BRUTUS

What said he when he came unto himself?

CASCA

Marry, before he fell down, when he perceived the common herd was glad he refused the crown, he plucked me ope his doublet and offered them his throat to cut. An I had been a man of any occupation, if I would not have taken him at a word, I would I might go to hell among the rogues. And so he fell. When he came to himself again, he said, If he had done or said anything amiss, he desired their worships to think it was his infirmity. Three or four wenches, where I stood, cried 'Alas, good soul!' and forgave him with all their hearts. But there's no heed to be taken of them; if Caesar had stabbed their mothers, they would have done no less.

BRUTUS

And after that, he came, thus sad, away?

CASCA

Ay.

CASSIUS

Did Cicero say anything?

CASCA

Ay, he spoke Greek.

CASSIUS

To what effect?

CASCA

Nay, an I tell you that, I'll ne'er look you i' the face again. But those that understood him smiled at one another and shook their heads; but, for mine own part, it was Greek to me. I could tell you more news too: Marullus and Flavius, for pulling scarfs off Caesar's images, are put to silence. Fare you well. There was more foolery yet, if I could remember it.

CASSIUS

Will you sup with me to-night, Casca?

CASCA

No, I am promised forth.

CASSIUS

Will you dine with me to-morrow?

CASCA

Ay, if I be alive and your mind hold and your dinner worth the eating.

CASSIUS

Good: I will expect you.

CASCA

Do so. Farewell, both.

Exit

BRUTUS

What a blunt fellow is this grown to be!
He was quick mettle when he went to school.

CASSIUS

So is he now in execution
Of any bold or noble enterprise,
However he puts on this tardy form.
This rudeness is a sauce to his good wit,
Which gives men stomach to digest his words
With better appetite.

BRUTUS

And so it is. For this time I will leave you:
To-morrow, if you please to speak with me,
I will come home to you; or, if you will,
Come home to me, and I will wait for you.

CASSIUS

I will do so: till then, think of the world.

Exit BRUTUS

Well, Brutus, thou art noble; yet, I see,
Thy honourable metal may be wrought
From that it is disposed. Therefore it is meet
That noble minds keep ever with their likes;
For who so firm that cannot be seduced?
Caesar doth bear me hard; but he loves Brutus.
If I were Brutus now and he were Cassius,
He should not humour me. I will this night,
In several hands, in at his windows throw,
As if they came from several citizens,
Writings all tending to the great opinion
That Rome holds of his name; wherein obscurely
Caesar's ambition shall be glanced at.
And after this let Caesar seat him sure;
For we will shake him, or worse days endure.

Exit

SCENE III. THE SAME. A STREET.

Thunder and lightning. Enter from opposite sides, CASCA, with his sword drawn, and CICERO

CICERO

Good even, Casca: brought you Caesar home?
Why are you breathless? and why stare you so?

CASCA

Are not you moved, when all the sway of earth
Shakes like a thing unfirm? O Cicero,
I have seen tempests, when the scolding winds
Have rived the knotty oaks, and I have seen
The ambitious ocean swell and rage and foam,
To be exalted with the threatening clouds;
But never till to-night, never till now,
Did I go through a tempest dropping fire.
Either there is a civil strife in heaven,
Or else the world, too saucy with the gods,
Incenses them to send destruction.

CICERO

Why, saw you anything more wonderful?

CASCA

A common slave—you know him well by sight—
Held up his left hand, which did flame and burn
Like twenty torches join'd, and yet his hand,
Not sensible of fire, remain'd unscorch'd.
Besides—I ha' not since put up my sword—
Against the Capitol I met a lion,

Who glared upon me, and went surly by,
Without annoying me: and there were drawn
Upon a heap a hundred ghastly women,
Transformed with their fear; who swore they saw
Men all in fire walk up and down the streets.
And yesterday the bird of night did sit
Even at noon-day upon the market-place,
Hooting and shrieking. When these prodigies
Do so conjointly meet, let not men say
'These are their reasons—they are natural,'
For, I believe, they are portentous things
Unto the climate that they point upon.

CICERO

Indeed, it is a strange-disposed time;
But men may construe things after their fashion,
Clean from the purpose of the things themselves.
Come Caesar to the Capitol to-morrow?

CASCA

He doth; for he did bid Antonius
Send word to you he would be there to-morrow.

CICERO

Good night then, Casca: this disturbed sky
Is not to walk in.

CASCA

Farewell, Cicero.

Exit CICERO

Enter CASSIUS

CASSIUS

Who's there?

CASCA

A Roman.

CASSIUS

Casca, by your voice.

CASCA

Your ear is good. Cassius, what night is this!

CASSIUS

A very pleasing night to honest men.

CASCA

Who ever knew the heavens menace so?

CASSIUS

Those that have known the earth so full of faults.
For my part, I have walk'd about the streets,
Submitting me unto the perilous night,
And, thus unbraced, Casca, as you see,
Have bared my bosom to the thunder-stone;
And when the cross blue lightning seem'd to open

The breast of heaven, I did present myself
Even in the aim and very flash of it.

CASCA

But wherefore did you so much tempt the
heavens?
It is the part of men to fear and tremble,
When the most mighty gods by tokens send
Such dreadful heralds to astonish us.

CASSIUS

You are dull, Casca, and those sparks of life
That should be in a Roman you do want,
Or else you use not. You look pale and gaze
And put on fear and cast yourself in wonder,
To see the strange impatience of the heavens:
But if you would consider the true cause
Why all these fires, why all these gliding ghosts,
Why birds and beasts from quality and kind,
Why old men fool and children calculate,
Why all these things change from their ordinance
Their natures and preformed faculties
To monstrous quality—why, you shall find
That heaven hath infused them with these spirits,
To make them instruments of fear and warning
Unto some monstrous state.

Now could I, Casca, name to thee a man
Most like this dreadful night,
That thunders, lightens, opens graves, and roars
As doth the lion in the Capitol;
A man no mightier than thyself or me
In personal action, yet prodigious grown,
And fearful, as these strange eruptions are.

CASCA

'Tis Caesar that you mean; is it not, Cassius?

CASSIUS

Let it be who it is: for Romans now
Have thews and limbs like to their ancestors.
But, woe the while! our fathers' minds are dead,
And we are govern'd with our mothers' spirits;
Our yoke and sufferance show us womanish.

CASCA

Indeed, they say the senators to-morrow
Mean to establish Caesar as a king;
And he shall wear his crown by sea and land,
In every place, save here in Italy.

CASSIUS

I know where I will wear this dagger then;
Cassius from bondage will deliver Cassius.
Therein, ye gods, you make the weak most strong;

Therein, ye gods, you tyrants do defeat.
Nor stony tower, nor walls of beaten brass,
Nor airless dungeon, nor strong links of iron,
Can be retentive to the strength of spirit;
But life, being weary of these worldly bars,
Never lacks power to dismiss itself.
If I know this, know all the world besides,
That part of tyranny that I do bear
I can shake off at pleasure.

Thunder still

CASCA

So can I;
So every bondman in his own hand bears
The power to cancel his captivity.

CASSIUS

And why should Caesar be a tyrant then?
Poor man! I know he would not be a wolf,
But that he sees the Romans are but sheep;
He were no lion, were not Romans hinds.
Those that with haste will make a mighty fire
Begin it with weak straws: what trash is Rome,
What rubbish and what offal, when it serves
For the base matter to illuminate
So vile a thing as Caesar! But, O grief,

Where hast thou led me? I perhaps speak this
Before a willing bondman; then I know
My answer must be made. But I am arm'd,
And dangers are to me indifferent.

CASCA

You speak to Casca, and to such a man
That is no fleering tell-tale. Hold, my hand:
Be factious for redress of all these griefs,
And I will set this foot of mine as far
As who goes farthest.

CASSIUS

There's a bargain made.
Now know you, Casca, I have moved already
Some certain of the noblest-minded Romans
To undergo with me an enterprise
Of honourable-dangerous consequence;
And I do know, by this, they stay for me
In Pompey's porch: for now, this fearful night,
There is no stir or walking in the streets;
And the complexion of the element
In favour's like the work we have in hand,
Most bloody, fiery, and most terrible.

CASCA

Stand close awhile, for here comes one in haste.

CASSIUS

'Tis Cinna; I do know him by his gait;
He is a friend.

Enter CINNA

Cinna, where haste you so?

CINNA

To find out you. Who's that? Metellus Cimber?

CASSIUS

No, it is Casca; one incorporate
To our attempts. Am I not stay'd for, Cinna?

CINNA

I am glad on't. What a fearful night is this!
There's two or three of us have seen strange sights.

CASSIUS

Am I not stay'd for? Tell me.

CINNA

Yes, you are. O Cassius, if you could
But win the noble Brutus to our party—

CASSIUS

Be you content: good Cinna, take this paper,
And look you lay it in the praetor's chair,
Where Brutus may but find it; and throw this
In at his window; set this up with wax
Upon old Brutus' statue: all this done,

Repair to Pompey's porch, where you shall find us.
Is Decius Brutus and Trebonius there?

CINNA

All but Metellus Cimber; and he's gone
To seek you at your house. Well, I will hie,
And so bestow these papers as you bade me.

CASSIUS

That done, repair to Pompey's theatre.

Exit CINNA

Come, Casca, you and I will yet ere day
See Brutus at his house: three parts of him
Is ours already, and the man entire
Upon the next encounter yields him ours.

CASCA

O, he sits high in all the people's hearts;
And that which would appear offence in us,
His countenance, like richest alchemy,
Will change to virtue and to worthiness.

CASSIUS

Him and his worth and our great need of him
You have right well conceited. Let us go,
For it is after midnight; and ere day
We will awake him and be sure of him.

Exeunt

Act 2

Scene I. Rome. BRUTUS's Orchard.

Enter BRUTUS

BRUTUS

What, Lucius, ho!

I cannot, by the progress of the stars,

Give guess how near to day. Lucius, I say!

I would it were my fault to sleep so soundly.

When, Lucius, when? awake, I say! what, Lucius!

Enter LUCIUS

LUCIUS

Call'd you, my lord?

BRUTUS

Get me a taper in my study, Lucius;

When it is lighted, come and call me here.

LUCIUS

I will, my lord.

Exit

BRUTUS

It must be by his death; and for my part,
I know no personal cause to spurn at him,
But for the general. He would be crown'd:
How that might change his nature, there's the question.
It is the bright day that brings forth the adder,
And that craves wary walking. Crown him—that!
And then, I grant, we put a sting in him
That at his will he may do danger with.
The abuse of greatness is, when it disjoins
Remorse from power: and, to speak truth of Caesar,
I have not known when his affections sway'd
More than his reason. But 'tis a common proof,
That lowliness is young ambition's ladder,
Whereto the climber-upward turns his face;
But when he once attains the upmost round.
He then unto the ladder turns his back,
Looks in the clouds, scorning the base degrees
By which he did ascend. So Caesar may.
Then, lest he may, prevent. And, since the quarrel
Will bear no colour for the thing he is,
Fashion it thus—that what he is, augmented,

Would run to these and these extremities;
And therefore think him as a serpent's egg
Which, hatch'd, would, as his kind, grow mischievous,
And kill him in the shell.

Re-enter LUCIUS

LUCIUS

The taper burneth in your closet, sir.
Searching the window for a flint, I found
This paper, thus seal'd up; and, I am sure,
It did not lie there when I went to bed.

Gives him the letter

BRUTUS

Get you to bed again; it is not day.
Is not to-morrow, boy, the ides of March?

LUCIUS

I know not, sir.

BRUTUS

Look in the calendar, and bring me word.

LUCIUS

I will, sir.

Exit

BRUTUS

The exhalations whizzing in the air

Give so much light that I may read by them.

Opens the letter and reads

'Brutus, thou sleep'st. Awake, and see thyself.
Shall Rome, &c. Speak, strike, redress!
Brutus, thou sleep'st; awake!'
Such instigations have been often dropp'd
Where I have took them up.
'Shall Rome, &c.' Thus must I piece it out:
Shall Rome stand under one man's awe? What,
Rome?
My ancestors did from the streets of Rome
The Tarquin drive, when he was call'd a king.
'Speak, strike, redress!' Am I entreated
To speak and strike? O Rome, I make thee
promise,
If the redress will follow, thou receivest
Thy full petition at the hand of Brutus!

Re-enter LUCIUS

LUCIUS

Sir, March is wasted fourteen days.

Knocking within

BRUTUS

'Tis good. Go to the gate; somebody knocks.

Exit LUCIUS

Since Cassius first did whet me against Caesar,
I have not slept.
Between the acting of a dreadful thing
And the first motion, all the interim is
Like a phantasma, or a hideous dream.
The Genius and the mortal instruments
Are then in council; and the state of man,
Like to a little kingdom, suffers then
The nature of an insurrection.

Re-enter LUCIUS

LUCIUS

Sir, 'tis your brother Cassius at the door,
Who doth desire to see you.

BRUTUS

Is he alone?

LUCIUS

No, sir, there are more with him.

BRUTUS

Do you know them?

LUCIUS

No, sir; their hats are pluck'd about their ears,
And half their faces buried in their cloaks,
That by no means I may discover them
By any mark of favour.

BRUTUS

Let 'em enter.

Exit LUCIUS

They are the faction. O conspiracy,
Shamest thou to show thy dangerous brow by night,
When evils are most free? O, then by day
Where wilt thou find a cavern dark enough
To mask thy monstrous visage? Seek none, conspiracy;
Hide it in smiles and affability!
For if thou path, thy native semblance on,
Not Erebus itself were dim enough
To hide thee from prevention.

Enter the conspirators, CASSIUS, CASCA, DECIUS BRUTUS, CINNA, METELLUS CIMBER, and TREBONIUS

CASSIUS

I think we are too bold upon your rest.
Good morrow, Brutus; do we trouble you?

BRUTUS

I have been up this hour, awake all night.
Know I these men that come along with you?

CASSIUS

Yes, every man of them, and no man here
But honours you; and every one doth wish
You had but that opinion of yourself
Which every noble Roman bears of you.
This is Trebonius.

BRUTUS

He is welcome hither.

CASSIUS

This, Decius Brutus.

BRUTUS

He is welcome too.

CASSIUS

This, Casca; this, Cinna; and this, Metellus
Cimber.

BRUTUS

They are all welcome.
What watchful cares do interpose themselves
Betwixt your eyes and night?

CASSIUS

Shall I entreat a word?

BRUTUS and CASSIUS whisper

DECIUS BRUTUS

Here lies the east. Doth not the day break here?

CASCA

No.

CINNA

O, pardon, sir, it doth; and yon grey lines
That fret the clouds are messengers of day.

CASCA

You shall confess that you are both deceived.
Here, as I point my sword, the sun arises,
Which is a great way growing on the south,
Weighing the youthful season of the year.
Some two months hence up higher toward the north
He first presents his fire; and the high east
Stands, as the Capitol, directly here.

BRUTUS

Give me your hands all over, one by one.

CASSIUS

And let us swear our resolution.

BRUTUS

No, not an oath: if not the face of men,
The sufferance of our souls, the time's abuse,
If these be motives weak, break off betimes,
And every man hence to his idle bed;
So let high-sighted tyranny range on,
Till each man drop by lottery. But if these,

As I am sure they do, bear fire enough
To kindle cowards and to steel with valour
The melting spirits of women, then, countrymen,
What need we any spur but our own cause,
To prick us to redress? what other bond
Than secret Romans, that have spoke the word,
And will not palter? and what other oath
Than honesty to honesty engaged,
That this shall be, or we will fall for it?
Swear priests and cowards and men cautelous,
Old feeble carrions and such suffering souls
That welcome wrongs; unto bad causes swear
Such creatures as men doubt; but do not stain
The even virtue of our enterprise,
Nor the insuppressive mettle of our spirits,
To think that or our cause or our performance
Did need an oath; when every drop of blood
That every Roman bears, and nobly bears,
Is guilty of a several bastardy,
If he do break the smallest particle
Of any promise that hath pass'd from him.

CASSIUS

But what of Cicero? Shall we sound him?
I think he will stand very strong with us.

CASCA

Let us not leave him out.

CINNA

No, by no means.

METELLUS CIMBER

O, let us have him, for his silver hairs
Will purchase us a good opinion
And buy men's voices to commend our deeds.
It shall be said, his judgment ruled our hands;
Our youths and wildness shall no whit appear,
But all be buried in his gravity.

BRUTUS

O, name him not! Let us not break with him;
For he will never follow anything
That other men begin.

CASSIUS

Then leave him out.

CASCA

Indeed he is not fit.

DECIUS BRUTUS

Shall no man else be touch'd but only Caesar?

CASSIUS

Decius, well urged: I think it is not meet,
Mark Antony, so well beloved of Caesar,

Should outlive Caesar: we shall find of him
A shrewd contriver; and, you know, his means,
If he improve them, may well stretch so far
As to annoy us all: which to prevent,
Let Antony and Caesar fall together.

BRUTUS

Our course will seem too bloody, Caius Cassius,
To cut the head off and then hack the limbs,
Like wrath in death and envy afterwards;
For Antony is but a limb of Caesar.
Let us be sacrificers, but not butchers, Caius.
We all stand up against the spirit of Caesar;
And in the spirit of men there is no blood.
O, that we then could come by Caesar's spirit,
And not dismember Caesar! But, alas,
Caesar must bleed for it! And, gentle friends,
Let's kill him boldly, but not wrathfully;
Let's carve him as a dish fit for the gods,
Not hew him as a carcass fit for hounds:
And let our hearts, as subtle masters do,
Stir up their servants to an act of rage,
And after seem to chide 'em. This shall make
Our purpose necessary and not envious:
Which so appearing to the common eyes,

We shall be call'd purgers, not murderers.
And for Mark Antony, think not of him;
For he can do no more than Caesar's arm
When Caesar's head is off.

CASSIUS

Yet I fear him;
For in the engrafted love he bears to Caesar—

BRUTUS

Alas, good Cassius, do not think of him!
If he love Caesar, all that he can do
Is to himself, take thought and die for Caesar;
And that were much he should; for he is given
To sports, to wildness and much company.

TREBONIUS

There is no fear in him; let him not die;
For he will live, and laugh at this hereafter.

Clock strikes

BRUTUS

Peace! Count the clock.

CASSIUS

The clock hath stricken three.

TREBONIUS

'Tis time to part.

CASSIUS

But it is doubtful yet,
Whether Caesar will come forth to-day, or no;
For he is superstitious grown of late,
Quite from the main opinion he held once
Of fantasy, of dreams and ceremonies:
It may be, these apparent prodigies,
The unaccustom'd terror of this night,
And the persuasion of his augurers,
May hold him from the Capitol to-day.

DECIUS BRUTUS

Never fear that: if he be so resolved,
I can o'ersway him; for he loves to hear
That unicorns may be betray'd with trees,
And bears with glasses, elephants with holes,
Lions with toils and men with flatterers;
But when I tell him he hates flatterers,
He says he does, being then most flattered.
Let me work;
For I can give his humour the true bent,
And I will bring him to the Capitol.

CASSIUS

Nay, we will all of us be there to fetch him.

BRUTUS

By the eighth hour: is that the uttermost?

CINNA

Be that the uttermost, and fail not then.

METELLUS CIMBER

Caius Ligarius doth bear Caesar hard,
Who rated him for speaking well of Pompey.
I wonder none of you have thought of him.

BRUTUS

Now, good Metellus, go along by him.
He loves me well, and I have given him reasons;
Send him but hither, and I'll fashion him.

CASSIUS

The morning comes upon's. We'll leave you, Brutus.
And, friends, disperse yourselves; but all remember
What you have said, and show yourselves true
Romans.

BRUTUS

Good gentlemen, look fresh and merrily;
Let not our looks put on our purposes,
But bear it as our Roman actors do,
With untired spirits and formal constancy.
And so good morrow to you every one.

Exeunt all but BRUTUS

Boy! Lucius! Fast asleep? It is no matter;
Enjoy the honey-heavy dew of slumber:
Thou hast no figures nor no fantasies,
Which busy care draws in the brains of men;
Therefore thou sleep'st so sound.

Enter PORTIA

PORTIA

Brutus, my lord!

BRUTUS

Portia, what mean you? Wherefore rise you now?
It is not for your health thus to commit
Your weak condition to the raw cold morning.

PORTIA

Nor for yours neither. You've ungently, Brutus,
Stole from my bed: and yesternight, at supper,
You suddenly arose, and walk'd about,
Musing and sighing, with your arms across,
And when I ask'd you what the matter was,
You stared upon me with ungentle looks;
I urged you further; then you scratch'd your head,
And too impatiently stamp'd with your foot.
Yet I insisted, yet you answer'd not,
But, with an angry wafture of your hand,
Gave sign for me to leave you: so I did;

Fearing to strengthen that impatience
Which seem'd too much enkindled, and withal
Hoping it was but an effect of humour,
Which sometime hath his hour with every man.
It will not let you eat, nor talk, nor sleep;
And could it work so much upon your shape
As it hath much prevail'd on your condition,
I should not know you, Brutus. Dear my lord,
Make me acquainted with your cause of grief.

BRUTUS

I am not well in health, and that is all.

PORTIA

Brutus is wise, and, were he not in health,
He would embrace the means to come by it.

BRUTUS

Why, so I do. Good Portia, go to bed.

PORTIA

Is Brutus sick, and is it physical
To walk unbraced and suck up the humours
Of the dank morning? What, is Brutus sick,
And will he steal out of his wholesome bed,
To dare the vile contagion of the night
And tempt the rheumy and unpurged air
To add unto his sickness? No, my Brutus;

You have some sick offence within your mind,
Which, by the right and virtue of my place,
I ought to know of: and, upon my knees,
I charm you, by my once-commended beauty,
By all your vows of love and that great vow
Which did incorporate and make us one,
That you unfold to me, yourself, your half,
Why you are heavy, and what men to-night
Have had to resort to you; for here have been
Some six or seven, who did hide their faces
Even from darkness.

BRUTUS

Kneel not, gentle Portia.

PORTIA

I should not need, if you were gentle Brutus.
Within the bond of marriage, tell me, Brutus,
Is it excepted I should know no secrets
That appertain to you? Am I yourself
But, as it were, in sort or limitation?
To keep with you at meals, comfort your bed,
And talk to you sometimes? Dwell I but in the suburbs
Of your good pleasure? If it be no more,
Portia is Brutus' harlot, not his wife.

BRUTUS

You are my true and honourable wife,
As dear to me as are the ruddy drops
That visit my sad heart.

PORTIA

If this were true, then should I know this secret.
I grant I am a woman; but withal
A woman that Lord Brutus took to wife.
I grant I am a woman; but withal
A woman well-reputed, Cato's daughter.
Think you I am no stronger than my sex,
Being so father'd and so husbanded?
Tell me your counsels, I will not disclose 'em.
I have made strong proof of my constancy,
Giving myself a voluntary wound
Here, in the thigh: can I bear that with patience.
And not my husband's secrets?

BRUTUS

O ye gods,
Render me worthy of this noble wife!

Knocking within

Hark, hark! one knocks. Portia, go in awhile;
And by and by thy bosom shall partake
The secrets of my heart.

All my engagements I will construe to thee,
All the charactery of my sad brows.
Leave me with haste.

Exit PORTIA

Lucius, who's that knocks?

Re-enter LUCIUS with LIGARIUS

LUCIUS

He is a sick man that would speak with you.

BRUTUS

Caius Ligarius, that Metellus spake of.
Boy, stand aside. Caius Ligarius, how?

LIGARIUS

Vouchsafe good morrow from a feeble tongue.

BRUTUS

O, what a time have you chose out, brave Caius,
To wear a kerchief! Would you were not sick!

LIGARIUS

I am not sick, if Brutus have in hand
Any exploit worthy the name of honour.

BRUTUS

Such an exploit have I in hand, Ligarius,
Had you a healthful ear to hear of it.

LIGARIUS

By all the gods that Romans bow before,

I here discard my sickness. [*Pulls off his kerchief*] Soul
of Rome!
Brave son, derived from honourable loins!
Thou, like an exorcist, hast conjured up
My mortified spirit. Now bid me run,
And I will strive with things impossible;
Yea, get the better of them. What's to do?

BRUTUS

A piece of work that will make sick men whole.

LIGARIUS

But are not some whole that we must make sick?

BRUTUS

That must we also. What it is, my Caius,
I shall unfold to thee, as we are going
To whom it must be done.

LIGARIUS

Set on your foot,
And with a heart new-fired I follow you,
To do I know not what; but it sufficeth
That Brutus leads me on. [*Thunder.*]

BRUTUS

Follow me, then.

Exeunt

SCENE II. CAESAR'S HOUSE.

Thunder and lightning. Enter CAESAR, in his night-gown

CAESAR

Nor heaven nor earth have been at peace to-night:
Thrice hath Calpurnia in her sleep cried out,
'Help, ho! They murder Caesar!' Who's within?

Enter a Servant

SERVANT

My lord?

CAESAR

Go bid the priests do present sacrifice
And bring me their opinions of success.

SERVANT

I will, my lord.

Exit

Enter CALPURNIA

CALPURNIA

What mean you, Caesar? Think you to walk forth?
You shall not stir out of your house to-day.

CAESAR

Caesar shall forth: the things that threaten'd me
Ne'er look'd but on my back. When they shall see
The face of Caesar, they are vanished.

CALPURNIA

Caesar, I never stood on ceremonies,
Yet now they fright me. There is one within,
Besides the things that we have heard and seen,
Recounts most horrid sights seen by the watch.
A lioness hath whelped in the streets;
And graves have yawn'd, and yielded up their dead;
Fierce fiery warriors fought upon the clouds,
In ranks and squadrons and right form of war,
Which drizzled blood upon the Capitol;
The noise of battle hurtled in the air,
Horses did neigh, and dying men did groan,
And ghosts did shriek and squeal about the streets.
O Caesar! these things are beyond all use,
And I do fear them.

CAESAR

What can be avoided
Whose end is purposed by the mighty gods?
Yet Caesar shall go forth; for these predictions
Are to the world in general as to Caesar.

CALPURNIA

When beggars die, there are no comets seen;
The heavens themselves blaze forth the death of princes.

CAESAR

Cowards die many times before their deaths;
The valiant never taste of death but once.
Of all the wonders that I yet have heard.
It seems to me most strange that men should fear;
Seeing that death, a necessary end,
Will come when it will come.

Re-enter Servant

What say the augurers?

SERVANT

They would not have you to stir forth to-day.
Plucking the entrails of an offering forth,
They could not find a heart within the beast.

CAESAR

The gods do this in shame of cowardice.
Caesar should be a beast without a heart,
If he should stay at home to-day for fear.
No, Caesar shall not: danger knows full well
That Caesar is more dangerous than he:
We are two lions litter'd in one day,
And I the elder and more terrible;
And Caesar shall go forth.

CALPURNIA

Alas, my lord,

Your wisdom is consumed in confidence.
Do not go forth to-day: call it my fear
That keeps you in the house, and not your own.
We'll send Mark Antony to the Senate House,
And he shall say you are not well to-day.
Let me, upon my knee, prevail in this.

CAESAR

Mark Antony shall say I am not well,
And, for thy humour, I will stay at home.

Enter DECIUS BRUTUS

Here's Decius Brutus, he shall tell them so.

DECIUS BRUTUS

Caesar, all hail! Good morrow, worthy Caesar.
I come to fetch you to the Senate House.

CAESAR

And you are come in very happy time,
To bear my greeting to the senators
And tell them that I will not come to-day.
Cannot, is false, and that I dare not, falser;
I will not come to-day: tell them so, Decius.

CALPURNIA

Say he is sick.

CAESAR

Shall Caesar send a lie?

Have I in conquest stretch'd mine arm so far,
To be afraid to tell greybeards the truth?
Decius, go tell them Caesar will not come.

DECIUS BRUTUS

Most mighty Caesar, let me know some cause,
Lest I be laugh'd at when I tell them so.

CAESAR

The cause is in my will: I will not come;
That is enough to satisfy the senate.
But for your private satisfaction,
Because I love you, I will let you know:
Calpurnia here, my wife, stays me at home.
She dreamt to-night she saw my statua,
Which, like a fountain with an hundred spouts,
Did run pure blood: and many lusty Romans
Came smiling, and did bathe their hands in it.
And these does she apply for warnings, and portents,
And evils imminent; and on her knee
Hath begg'd that I will stay at home to-day.

DECIUS BRUTUS

This dream is all amiss interpreted;
It was a vision fair and fortunate.
Your statue spouting blood in many pipes,

In which so many smiling Romans bathed,
Signifies that from you great Rome shall suck
Reviving blood, and that great men shall press
For tinctures, stains, relics and cognizance.
This by Calpurnia's dream is signified.

CAESAR

And this way have you well expounded it.

DECIUS BRUTUS

I have, when you have heard what I can say—
And know it now: the senate have concluded
To give this day a crown to mighty Caesar.
If you shall send them word you will not come,
Their minds may change. Besides, it were a mock
Apt to be render'd, for some one to say
'Break up the senate till another time,
When Caesar's wife shall meet with better
dreams.'
If Caesar hide himself, shall they not whisper
'Lo, Caesar is afraid'?
Pardon me, Caesar; for my dear dear love
To our proceeding bids me tell you this;
And reason to my love is liable.

CAESAR

How foolish do your fears seem now, Calpurnia!

I am ashamed I did yield to them.

Give me my robe, for I will go.

Enter PUBLIUS, BRUTUS, LIGARIUS, METELLUS, CASCA, TREBONIUS, and CINNA

And look where Publius is come to fetch me.

PUBLIUS

Good morrow, Caesar.

CAESAR

Welcome, Publius.

What, Brutus, are you stirr'd so early too?

Good morrow, Casca. Caius Ligarius,

Caesar was ne'er so much your enemy

As that same ague which hath made you lean.

What is't o'clock?

BRUTUS

Caesar, 'tis strucken eight.

CAESAR

I thank you for your pains and courtesy.

Enter ANTONY

See! Antony, that revels long o' nights,

Is notwithstanding up. Good morrow, Antony.

ANTONY

So to most noble Caesar.

CAESAR

Bid them prepare within.
I am to blame to be thus waited for.
Now, Cinna. Now, Metellus. What, Trebonius!
I have an hour's talk in store for you.
Remember that you call on me to-day;
Be near me, that I may remember you.

TREBONIUS

Caesar, I will.

[*Aside*]

And so near will I be,
That your best friends shall wish I had been
further.

CAESAR

Good friends, go in, and taste some wine with me;
And we, like friends, will straightway go together.

BRUTUS

[*Aside*] That every like is not the same, O Caesar,
The heart of Brutus yearns to think upon!

Exeunt

Scene III. A Street Near The Capitol.

Enter ARTEMIDORUS, reading a paper

ARTEMIDORUS

'Caesar, beware of Brutus; take heed of Cassius; come not near Casca; have an eye to Cinna; trust not Trebonius; mark well Metellus Cimber; Decius Brutus loves thee not; thou hast wronged Caius Ligarius. There is but one mind in all these men, and it is bent against Caesar. If thou beest not immortal, look about you. Security gives way to conspiracy. The mighty gods defend thee!

Thy lover,

'ARTEMIDORUS.'

Here will I stand till Caesar pass along,
And as a suitor will I give him this.
My heart laments that virtue cannot live
Out of the teeth of emulation.
If thou read this, O Caesar, thou mayst live;
If not, the Fates with traitors do contrive.

Exit

Scene IV. Another Part of The Same Street, Before The House of Brutus.

Enter PORTIA and LUCIUS

PORTIA

I prithee, boy, run to the Senate House;
Stay not to answer me, but get thee gone.
Why dost thou stay?

LUCIUS

To know my errand, madam.

PORTIA

I would have had thee there, and here again,
Ere I can tell thee what thou shouldst do there.
O constancy, be strong upon my side!
Set a huge mountain 'tween my heart and tongue!
I have a man's mind, but a woman's might.
How hard it is for women to keep counsel!
Art thou here yet?

LUCIUS

Madam, what should I do?
Run to the Capitol, and nothing else?
And so return to you, and nothing else?

PORTIA

Yes, bring me word, boy, if thy lord look well,

For he went sickly forth: and take good note
What Caesar doth, what suitors press to him.
Hark, boy! what noise is that?

LUCIUS

I hear none, madam.

PORTIA

Prithee, listen well.
I heard a bustling rumour, like a fray,
And the wind brings it from the Capitol.

LUCIUS

Sooth, madam, I hear nothing.

Enter the Soothsayer

PORTIA

Come hither, fellow. Which way hast thou been?

SOOTHSAYER

At mine own house, good lady.

PORTIA

What is't o'clock?

SOOTHSAYER

About the ninth hour, lady.

PORTIA

Is Caesar yet gone to the Capitol?

SOOTHSAYER

Madam, not yet: I go to take my stand,

To see him pass on to the Capitol.

PORTIA

Thou hast some suit to Caesar, hast thou not?

SOOTHSAYER

That I have, lady. If it will please Caesar
To be so good to Caesar as to hear me,
I shall beseech him to befriend himself.

PORTIA

Why, know'st thou any harm's intended towards him?

SOOTHSAYER

None that I know will be, much that I fear may chance.
Good morrow to you. Here the street is narrow;
The throng that follows Caesar at the heels,
Of senators, of praetors, common suitors,
Will crowd a feeble man almost to death.
I'll get me to a place more void, and there
Speak to great Caesar as he comes along.

Exit

PORTIA

I must go in. Ay me, how weak a thing
The heart of woman is! O Brutus,
The heavens speed thee in thine enterprise!

Sure, the boy heard me: Brutus hath a suit
That Caesar will not grant. O, I grow faint.
Run, Lucius, and commend me to my lord;
Say I am merry: come to me again,
And bring me word what he doth say to thee.

Exeunt severally

Act 3

Scene I. Rome. Before the Capitol; the Senate sitting above.

A crowd of people; among them ARTEMIDORUS and the Soothsayer. Flourish. Enter CAESAR, BRUTUS, CASSIUS, CASCA, DECIUS BRUTUS, METELLUS CIMBER, TREBONIUS, CINNA, ANTONY, LEPIDUS, POPILIUS, PUBLIUS, and others

CAESAR

[*To the Soothsayer*] The ides of March are come.

SOOTHSAYER

Ay, Caesar; but not gone.

ARTEMIDORUS

Hail, Caesar! Read this schedule.

DECIUS BRUTUS

Trebonius doth desire you to o'erread,
At your best leisure, this his humble suit.

ARTEMIDORUS

O Caesar, read mine first; for mine's a suit
That touches Caesar nearer. Read it, great Caesar.

CAESAR

What touches us ourself shall be last served.

ARTEMIDORUS

Delay not, Caesar; read it instantly.

CAESAR

What, is the fellow mad?

PUBLIUS

Sirrah, give place.

CASSIUS

What, urge you your petitions in the street?
Come to the Capitol.

CAESAR goes up to the Senate House, the rest following

POPILIUS

I wish your enterprise to-day may thrive.

CASSIUS

What enterprise, Popilius?

POPILIUS

Fare you well.

Advances to CAESAR

BRUTUS

What said Popilius Lena?

CASSIUS

He wish'd to-day our enterprise might thrive.
I fear our purpose is discovered.

BRUTUS

Look, how he makes to Caesar; mark him.

CASSIUS

Casca, be sudden, for we fear prevention.
Brutus, what shall be done? If this be known,
Cassius or Caesar never shall turn back,
For I will slay myself.

BRUTUS

Cassius, be constant.
Popilius Lena speaks not of our purposes;
For, look, he smiles, and Caesar doth not change.

CASSIUS

Trebonius knows his time; for, look you, Brutus.
He draws Mark Antony out of the way.

Exeunt ANTONY and TREBONIUS

DECIUS BRUTUS

Where is Metellus Cimber? Let him go,
And presently prefer his suit to Caesar.

BRUTUS

He is address'd; press near and second him.

CINNA

Casca, you are the first that rears your hand.

CAESAR

Are we all ready? What is now amiss
That Caesar and his senate must redress?

METELLUS CIMBER

Most high, most mighty, and most puissant Caesar,
Metellus Cimber throws before thy seat
An humble heart.

Kneeling

CAESAR

I must prevent thee, Cimber.
These couchings and these lowly courtesies
Might fire the blood of ordinary men,
And turn pre-ordinance and first decree
Into the law of children. Be not fond,
To think that Caesar bears such rebel blood
That will be thaw'd from the true quality
With that which melteth fools; I mean, sweet words,
Low-crooked court'sies and base spaniel-fawning.
Thy brother by decree is banished:

If thou dost bend and pray and fawn for him,
I spurn thee like a cur out of my way.
Know, Caesar doth not wrong, nor without
cause
Will he be satisfied.

METELLUS CIMBER

Is there no voice more worthy than my own
To sound more sweetly in great Caesar's ear
For the repealing of my banish'd brother?

BRUTUS

I kiss thy hand, but not in flattery, Caesar;
Desiring thee that Publius Cimber may
Have an immediate freedom of repeal.

CAESAR

What, Brutus!

CASSIUS

Pardon, Caesar! Caesar, pardon!
As low as to thy foot doth Cassius fall,
To beg enfranchisement for Publius Cimber.

CASSIUS

I could be well moved, if I were as you;
If I could pray to move, prayers would move me;
But I am constant as the northern star,
Of whose true-fix'd and resting quality

There is no fellow in the firmament.
The skies are painted with unnumber'd sparks,
They are all fire and every one doth shine,
But there's but one in all doth hold his place.
So in the world; 'tis furnish'd well with men,
And men are flesh and blood, and apprehensive;
Yet in the number I do know but one
That unassailable holds on his rank,
Unshaked of motion: and that I am he,
Let me a little show it, even in this;
That I was constant Cimber should be banish'd,
And constant do remain to keep him so.

CINNA

O Caesar!

CAESAR

Hence! Wilt thou lift up Olympus?

DECIUS BRUTUS

Great Caesar!

CAESAR

Doth not Brutus bootless kneel?

CASCA

Speak, hands for me!

CASCA first, then the other
Conspirators and BRUTUS stab CAESAR

CAESAR

Et tu, Brute! Then fall, Caesar.

Dies

CINNA

Liberty! Freedom! Tyranny is dead!

Run hence, proclaim, cry it about the streets.

CASSIUS

Some to the common pulpits, and cry out

'Liberty, freedom, and enfranchisement!'

BRUTUS

People and senators, be not affrighted.

Fly not; stand stiff. Ambition's debt is paid.

CASCA

Go to the pulpit, Brutus.

DECIUS BRUTUS

And Cassius too.

BRUTUS

Where's Publius?

CINNA

Here, quite confounded with this mutiny.

METELLUS CIMBER

Stand fast together, lest some friend of Caesar's

Should chance—

BRUTUS

Talk not of standing. Publius, good cheer!
There is no harm intended to your person,
Nor to no Roman else: so tell them, Publius.

CASSIUS

And leave us, Publius; lest that the people,
Rushing on us, should do your age some mischief.

BRUTUS

Do so: and let no man abide this deed,
But we the doers.

Re-enter TREBONIUS

CASSIUS

Where is Antony?

TREBONIUS

Fled to his house amazed.
Men, wives and children stare, cry out and run
As it were doomsday.

BRUTUS

Fates, we will know your pleasures.
That we shall die, we know; 'tis but the time
And drawing days out, that men stand upon.

CASSIUS

Why, he that cuts off twenty years of life
Cuts off so many years of fearing death.

BRUTUS

Grant that, and then is death a benefit.
So are we Caesar's friends, that have abridged
His time of fearing death. Stoop, Romans, stoop,
And let us bathe our hands in Caesar's blood
Up to the elbows, and besmear our swords.
Then walk we forth, even to the market-place,
And, waving our red weapons o'er our heads,
Let's all cry 'Peace, freedom and liberty!'

CASSIUS

Stoop, then, and wash. How many ages hence
Shall this our lofty scene be acted over
In states unborn and accents yet unknown!

BRUTUS

How many times shall Caesar bleed in sport,
That now on Pompey's basis lies along
No worthier than the dust!

CASSIUS

So oft as that shall be,
So often shall the knot of us be call'd
The men that gave their country liberty.

DECIUS BRUTUS

What, shall we forth?

CASSIUS

Ay, every man away.
Brutus shall lead; and we will grace his heels
With the most boldest and best hearts of Rome.

Enter a Servant

BRUTUS

Soft! who comes here? A friend of Antony's.

SERVANT

Thus, Brutus, did my master bid me kneel;
Thus did Mark Antony bid me fall down;
And, being prostrate, thus he bade me say:
Brutus is noble, wise, valiant, and honest;
Caesar was mighty, bold, royal, and loving.
Say I love Brutus, and I honour him;
Say I fear'd Caesar, honour'd him and loved him.
If Brutus will vouchsafe that Antony
May safely come to him, and be resolved
How Caesar hath deserved to lie in death,
Mark Antony shall not love Caesar dead
So well as Brutus living; but will follow
The fortunes and affairs of noble Brutus
Thorough the hazards of this untrod state
With all true faith. So says my master Antony.

BRUTUS

Thy master is a wise and valiant Roman;
I never thought him worse.
Tell him, so please him come unto this place,
He shall be satisfied; and, by my honour,
Depart untouch'd.

SERVANT

I'll fetch him presently.

Exit

BRUTUS

I know that we shall have him well to friend.

CASSIUS

I wish we may: but yet have I a mind
That fears him much; and my misgiving still
Falls shrewdly to the purpose.

BRUTUS

But here comes Antony.

Re-enter ANTONY

Welcome, Mark Antony.

ANTONY

O mighty Caesar! dost thou lie so low?
Are all thy conquests, glories, triumphs, spoils,
Shrunk to this little measure? Fare thee well.
I know not, gentlemen, what you intend,

Who else must be let blood, who else is rank:
If I myself, there is no hour so fit
As Caesar's death hour, nor no instrument
Of half that worth as those your swords, made rich
With the most noble blood of all this world.
I do beseech ye, if you bear me hard,
Now, whilst your purpled hands do reek and smoke,
Fulfil your pleasure. Live a thousand years,
I shall not find myself so apt to die.
No place will please me so, no mean of death,
As here by Caesar, and by you cut off,
The choice and master spirits of this age.

BRUTUS

O Antony! beg not your death of us.
Though now we must appear bloody and cruel,
As, by our hands and this our present act,
You see we do, yet see you but our hands
And this the bleeding business they have done:
Our hearts you see not; they are pitiful;
And pity to the general wrong of Rome—
As fire drives out fire, so pity pity—
Hath done this deed on Caesar. For your part,

To you our swords have leaden points, Mark
Antony:
Our arms, in strength of malice, and our hearts
Of brothers' temper, do receive you in
With all kind love, good thoughts, and reverence.

CASSIUS

Your voice shall be as strong as any man's
In the disposing of new dignities.

BRUTUS

Only be patient till we have appeased
The multitude, beside themselves with fear,
And then we will deliver you the cause,
Why I, that did love Caesar when I struck him,
Have thus proceeded.

ANTONY

I doubt not of your wisdom.
Let each man render me his bloody hand:
First, Marcus Brutus, will I shake with you;
Next, Caius Cassius, do I take your hand;
Now, Decius Brutus, yours: now yours, Metellus;
Yours, Cinna; and, my valiant Casca, yours.
Though last, not last in love, yours, good
Trebonius.
Gentlemen all—alas, what shall I say?

My credit now stands on such slippery ground,
That one of two bad ways you must conceit me,
Either a coward or a flatterer.
That I did love thee, Caesar, O, 'tis true!
If then thy spirit look upon us now,
Shall it not grieve thee dearer than thy death,
To see thy thy Anthony making his peace,
Shaking the bloody fingers of thy foes,
Most noble! in the presence of thy corse?
Had I as many eyes as thou hast wounds,
Weeping as fast as they stream forth thy blood,
It would become me better than to close
In terms of friendship with thine enemies.
Pardon me, Julius! Here wast thou bay'd, brave hart;
Here didst thou fall; and here thy hunters stand,
Sign'd in thy spoil, and crimson'd in thy lethe.
O world, thou wast the forest to this hart;
And this, indeed, O world, the heart of thee!
How like a deer, strucken by many princes,
Dost thou here lie!

CASSIUS

Mark Antony—

ANTONY

Pardon me, Caius Cassius.

The enemies of Caesar shall say this;
Then, in a friend, it is cold modesty.

CASSIUS

I blame you not for praising Caesar so;
But what compact mean you to have with us?
Will you be prick'd in number of our friends,
Or shall we on, and not depend on you?

ANTONY

Therefore I took your hands, but was, indeed,
Sway'd from the point, by looking down on Caesar.
Friends am I with you all and love you all,
Upon this hope, that you shall give me reasons
Why and wherein Caesar was dangerous.

BRUTUS

Or else were this a savage spectacle.
Our reasons are so full of good regard
That were you, Antony, the son of Caesar,
You should be satisfied.

ANTONY

That's all I seek;
And am moreover suitor that I may
Produce his body to the market-place;
And in the pulpit, as becomes a friend,
Speak in the order of his funeral.

BRUTUS

You shall, Mark Antony.

CASSIUS

Brutus, a word with you.

Aside to BRUTUS

You know not what you do. Do not consent
That Antony speak in his funeral.
Know you how much the people may be moved
By that which he will utter?

BRUTUS

By your pardon;
I will myself into the pulpit first,
And show the reason of our Caesar's death.
What Antony shall speak, I will protest
He speaks by leave and by permission,
And that we are contented Caesar shall
Have all true rites and lawful ceremonies.
It shall advantage more than do us wrong.

CASSIUS

I know not what may fall; I like it not.

BRUTUS

Mark Antony, here, take you Caesar's body.
You shall not in your funeral speech blame us,
But speak all good you can devise of Caesar,

And say you do't by our permission;
Else shall you not have any hand at all
About his funeral: and you shall speak
In the same pulpit whereto I am going,
After my speech is ended.

ANTONY

Be it so.
I do desire no more.

BRUTUS

Prepare the body then, and follow us.

Exeunt all but ANTONY

ANTONY

O, pardon me, thou bleeding piece of earth,
That I am meek and gentle with these butchers!
Thou art the ruins of the noblest man
That ever lived in the tide of times.
Woe to the hand that shed this costly blood!
Over thy wounds now do I prophesy—
Which, like dumb mouths, do ope their ruby lips,
To beg the voice and utterance of my tongue—
A curse shall light upon the limbs of men;
Domestic fury and fierce civil strife
Shall cumber all the parts of Italy;
Blood and destruction shall be so in use

And dreadful objects so familiar
That mothers shall but smile when they behold
Their infants quarter'd with the hands of war;
All pity choked with custom of fell deeds;
And Caesar's spirit, ranging for revenge,
With Ate by his side come hot from hell,
Shall in these confines with a monarch's voice
Cry 'Havoc,' and let slip the dogs of war;
That this foul deed shall smell above the earth
With carrion men, groaning for burial.

Enter a Servant

You serve Octavius Caesar, do you not?

SERVANT

I do, Mark Antony.

ANTONY

Caesar did write for him to come to Rome.

SERVANT

He did receive his letters, and is coming;
And bid me say to you by word of mouth—
O Caesar!

Seeing the body

ANTONY

Thy heart is big, get thee apart and weep.
Passion, I see, is catching; for mine eyes,

Seeing those beads of sorrow stand in thine,
Began to water. Is thy master coming?

SERVANT

He lies to-night within seven leagues of Rome.

ANTONY

Post back with speed, and tell him what hath chanced:
Here is a mourning Rome, a dangerous Rome,
No Rome of safety for Octavius yet;
Hie hence, and tell him so. Yet, stay awhile;
Thou shalt not back till I have borne this corse
Into the market-place: there shall I try
In my oration, how the people take
The cruel issue of these bloody men;
According to the which, thou shalt discourse
To young Octavius of the state of things.
Lend me your hand.

Exeunt with CAESAR's body

SCENE II. THE FORUM.

Enter BRUTUS and CASSIUS, and a throng of Citizens

CITIZENS

We will be satisfied! Let us be satisfied!

BRUTUS

Then follow me, and give me audience, friends.
Cassius, go you into the other street,
And part the numbers.
Those that will hear me speak, let 'em stay here;
Those that will follow Cassius, go with him;
And public reasons shall be rendered
Of Caesar's death.

FIRST CITIZEN

I will hear Brutus speak.

SECOND CITIZEN

I will hear Cassius; and compare their reasons,
When severally we hear them rendered.

Exit CASSIUS, with some of the Citizens.

BRUTUS goes into the pulpit

THIRD CITIZEN

The noble Brutus is ascended. Silence!

BRUTUS

Be patient till the last.

Romans, countrymen, and lovers! hear me for my cause, and be silent, that you may hear. Believe me for mine honour, and have respect to mine honour, that you may believe. Censure me in your wisdom, and awake your senses, that you may the better judge.

If there be any in this assembly, any dear friend of Caesar's, to him I say, that Brutus' love to Caesar was no less than his. If then that friend demand why Brutus rose against Caesar, this is my answer: Not that I loved Caesar less, but that I loved Rome more. Had you rather Caesar were living and die all slaves, than that Caesar were dead, to live all free men? As Caesar loved me, I weep for him; as he was fortunate, I rejoice at it; as he was valiant, I honour him; but, as he was ambitious, I slew him. There is tears for his love; joy for his fortune; honour for his valour; and death for his ambition. Who is here so base that would be a bondman? If any, speak; for him have I offended. Who is here so rude that would not be a Roman? If any, speak; for him have I offended. Who is here so vile that will not love his country? If any, speak; for him have I offended. I pause for a reply.

ALL

None, Brutus, none.

BRUTUS

Then none have I offended. I have done no more to Caesar than you shall do to Brutus. The question of his death is enrolled in the Capitol; his glory not extenuated, wherein he was worthy, nor his offences enforced, for which he suffered death.

Enter ANTONY and others, with CAESAR's body

Here comes his body, mourned by Mark Antony: who, though he had no hand in his death, shall receive the benefit of his dying, a place in the commonwealth; as which of you shall not? With this I depart—that, as I slew my best lover for the good of Rome, I have the same dagger for myself, when it shall please my country to need my death.

ALL

Live, Brutus! live, live!

FIRST CITIZEN

Bring him with triumph home unto his house.

SECOND CITIZEN

Give him a statue with his ancestors.

THIRD CITIZEN

Let him be Caesar.

FOURTH CITIZEN

Caesar's better parts
Shall be crown'd in Brutus.

FIRST CITIZEN

We'll bring him to his house with shouts and clamours.

BRUTUS

My countrymen—

SECOND CITIZEN

Peace, silence! Brutus speaks.

FIRST CITIZEN

Peace, ho!

BRUTUS

Good countrymen, let me depart alone,
And, for my sake, stay here with Antony.
Do grace to Caesar's corpse, and grace his speech
Tending to Caesar's glories; which Mark Antony,
By our permission, is allow'd to make.
I do entreat you, not a man depart,
Save I alone, till Antony have spoke.

Exit

FIRST CITIZEN

Stay, ho! and let us hear Mark Antony.

THIRD CITIZEN

Let him go up into the public chair;
We'll hear him. Noble Antony, go up.

ANTONY

For Brutus' sake, I am beholding to you.

Goes into the pulpit

FOURTH CITIZEN

What does he say of Brutus?

THIRD CITIZEN

He says, for Brutus' sake,

He finds himself beholding to us all.

FOURTH CITIZEN

'Twere best he speak no harm of Brutus here.

FIRST CITIZEN

This Caesar was a tyrant.

THIRD CITIZEN

Nay, that's certain.

We are blest that Rome is rid of him.

SECOND CITIZEN

Peace! let us hear what Antony can say.

ANTONY

You gentle Romans—

CITIZENS

Peace, ho! let us hear him.

ANTONY

Friends, Romans, countrymen, lend me your ears;

I come to bury Caesar, not to praise him.

The evil that men do lives after them;

The good is oft interred with their bones;

So let it be with Caesar. The noble Brutus

Hath told you Caesar was ambitious.
If it were so, it was a grievous fault,
And grievously hath Caesar answer'd it.
Here, under leave of Brutus and the rest—
For Brutus is an honourable man;
So are they all, all honourable men—
Come I to speak in Caesar's funeral.
He was my friend, faithful and just to me;
But Brutus says he was ambitious;
And Brutus is an honourable man.
He hath brought many captives home to Rome
Whose ransoms did the general coffers fill;
Did this in Caesar seem ambitious?
When that the poor have cried, Caesar hath wept;
Ambition should be made of sterner stuff.
Yet Brutus says he was ambitious;
And Brutus is an honourable man.
You all did see that on the Lupercal
I thrice presented him a kingly crown,
Which he did thrice refuse: was this ambition?
Yet Brutus says he was ambitious;
And, sure, he is an honourable man.
I speak not to disprove what Brutus spoke,
But here I am to speak what I do know.

You all did love him once, not without cause;
What cause withholds you then, to mourn for him?
O judgment! thou art fled to brutish beasts,
And men have lost their reason. Bear with me;
My heart is in the coffin there with Caesar,
And I must pause till it come back to me.

FIRST CITIZEN

Methinks there is much reason in his sayings.

SECOND CITIZEN

If thou consider rightly of the matter,
Caesar has had great wrong.

THIRD CITIZEN

Has he, masters?
I fear there will a worse come in his place.

FOURTH CITIZEN

Mark'd ye his words? He would not take the crown;
Therefore 'tis certain he was not ambitious.

FIRST CITIZEN

If it be found so, some will dear abide it.

SECOND CITIZEN

Poor soul! his eyes are red as fire with weeping.

THIRD CITIZEN

There's not a nobler man in Rome than Antony.

FOURTH CITIZEN

Now mark him, he begins again to speak.

ANTONY

But yesterday the word of Caesar might
Have stood against the world; now lies he there.
And none so poor to do him reverence.
O masters, if I were disposed to stir
Your hearts and minds to mutiny and rage,
I should do Brutus wrong, and Cassius wrong,
Who, you all know, are honourable men.
I will not do them wrong; I rather choose
To wrong the dead, to wrong myself and you,
Than I will wrong such honourable men.
But here's a parchment with the seal of Caesar;
I found it in his closet, 'tis his will.
Let but the commons hear this testament—
Which, pardon me, I do not mean to read—
And they would go and kiss dead Caesar's
wounds
And dip their napkins in his sacred blood,
Yea, beg a hair of him for memory,
And, dying, mention it within their wills,
Bequeathing it as a rich legacy
Unto their issue.

FOURTH CITIZEN

We'll hear the will: read it, Mark Antony.

ALL

The will, the will! We will hear Caesar's will.

ANTONY

Have patience, gentle friends, I must not read it;
It is not meet you know how Caesar loved you.
You are not wood, you are not stones, but men;
And, being men, bearing the will of Caesar,
It will inflame you, it will make you mad:
'Tis good you know not that you are his heirs;
For, if you should, O, what would come of it!

FOURTH CITIZEN

Read the will; we'll hear it, Antony;
You shall read us the will, Caesar's will.

ANTONY

Will you be patient? Will you stay awhile?
I have o'ershot myself to tell you of it:
I fear I wrong the honourable men
Whose daggers have stabb'd Caesar; I do fear it.

FOURTH CITIZEN

They were traitors: honourable men!

ALL

The will! the testament!

SECOND CITIZEN

They were villains, murderers: the will! Read the will.

ANTONY

You will compel me, then, to read the will?
Then make a ring about the corpse of Caesar,
And let me show you him that made the will.
Shall I descend? and will you give me leave?

SEVERAL CITIZENS

Come down.

SECOND CITIZEN

Descend.

THIRD CITIZEN

You shall have leave.

ANTONY comes down

FOURTH CITIZEN

A ring! Stand round.

FIRST CITIZEN

Stand from the hearse, stand from the body.

SECOND CITIZEN

Room for Antony, most noble Antony.

ANTONY

Nay, press not so upon me; stand far off.

SEVERAL CITIZENS

Stand back. Room! bear back.

ANTONY

If you have tears, prepare to shed them now.
You all do know this mantle: I remember
The first time ever Caesar put it on;
'Twas on a summer's evening, in his tent,
That day he overcame the Nervii.
Look, in this place ran Cassius' dagger through;
See what a rent the envious Casca made;
Through this the well-beloved Brutus stabb'd;
And as he pluck'd his cursed steel away,
Mark how the blood of Caesar follow'd it,
As rushing out of doors, to be resolved
If Brutus so unkindly knock'd, or no;
For Brutus, as you know, was Caesar's angel:
Judge, O you gods, how dearly Caesar loved him!
This was the most unkindest cut of all;
For when the noble Caesar saw him stab,
Ingratitude, more strong than traitors' arms,
Quite vanquish'd him: then burst his mighty heart;
And, in his mantle muffling up his face,
Even at the base of Pompey's statua,

Which all the while ran blood, great Caesar fell.
O, what a fall was there, my countrymen!
Then I, and you, and all of us fell down,
Whilst bloody treason flourish'd over us.
O, now you weep; and, I perceive, you feel
The dint of pity. These are gracious drops.
Kind souls, what, weep you when you but behold
Our Caesar's vesture wounded? Look you here,
Here is himself, marr'd, as you see, with traitors.

FIRST CITIZEN

O piteous spectacle!

SECOND CITIZEN

O noble Caesar!

THIRD CITIZEN

O woeful day!

FOURTH CITIZEN

O traitors, villains!

FIRST CITIZEN

O most bloody sight!

SECOND CITIZEN

We will be revenged.

ALL

Revenge! About! Seek! Burn! Fire! Kill! Slay!
Let not a traitor live!

ANTONY

Stay, countrymen.

FIRST CITIZEN

Peace there! Hear the noble Antony.

SECOND CITIZEN

We'll hear him, we'll follow him, we'll die with him.

ANTONY

Good friends, sweet friends, let me not stir you up
To such a sudden flood of mutiny.
They that have done this deed are honourable:
What private griefs they have, alas, I know not,
That made them do it: they are wise and honourable,
And will, no doubt, with reasons answer you.
I come not, friends, to steal away your hearts:
I am no orator, as Brutus is;
But, as you know me all, a plain blunt man,
That love my friend; and that they know full well
That gave me public leave to speak of him:
For I have neither wit, nor words, nor worth,
Action, nor utterance, nor the power of speech,
To stir men's blood: I only speak right on;
I tell you that which you yourselves do know;

Show you sweet Caesar's wounds, poor poor dumb mouths,
And bid them speak for me: but were I Brutus,
And Brutus Antony, there were an Antony
Would ruffle up your spirits and put a tongue
In every wound of Caesar that should move
The stones of Rome to rise and mutiny.

ALL

We'll mutiny.

FIRST CITIZEN

We'll burn the house of Brutus.

THIRD CITIZEN

Away, then! Come, seek the conspirators.

ANTONY

Yet hear me, countrymen; yet hear me speak.

ALL

Peace, ho! Hear Antony. Most noble Antony!

ANTONY

Why, friends, you go to do you know not what:
Wherein hath Caesar thus deserved your loves?
Alas, you know not: I must tell you then:
You have forgot the will I told you of.

ALL

Most true. The will! Let's stay and hear the will.

ANTONY

Here is the will, and under Caesar's seal.
To every Roman citizen he gives,
To every several man, seventy-five drachmas.

SECOND CITIZEN

Most noble Caesar! We'll revenge his death.

THIRD CITIZEN

O royal Caesar!

ANTONY

Hear me with patience.

ALL

Peace, ho!

ANTONY

Moreover, he hath left you all his walks,
His private arbours and new-planted orchards,
On this side Tiber; he hath left them you,
And to your heirs for ever, common pleasures,
To walk abroad, and recreate yourselves.
Here was a Caesar! When comes such another?

FIRST CITIZEN

Never, never! Come, away, away!
We'll burn his body in the holy place,
And with the brands fire the traitors' houses.
Take up the body.

SECOND CITIZEN

Go fetch fire.

THIRD CITIZEN

Pluck down benches.

FOURTH CITIZEN

Pluck down forms, windows, anything.

Exeunt CITIZENS with the body

ANTONY

Now let it work. Mischief, thou art afoot,
Take thou what course thou wilt!

Enter a Servant

How now, fellow!

SERVANT

Sir, Octavius is already come to Rome.

ANTONY

Where is he?

SERVANT

He and Lepidus are at Caesar's house.

ANTONY

And thither will I straight to visit him.
He comes upon a wish. Fortune is merry,
And in this mood will give us anything.

SERVANT

I heard him say, Brutus and Cassius
Are rid like madmen through the gates of Rome.

ANTONY

Belike they had some notice of the people,
How I had moved them. Bring me to Octavius.

Exeunt

SCENE III. A STREET.

Enter CINNA the Poet

CINNA THE POET

I dreamt to-night that I did feast with Caesar,
And things unlucky charge my fantasy.
I have no will to wander forth of doors,
Yet something leads me forth.

Enter Citizens

FIRST CITIZEN

What is your name?

SECOND CITIZEN

Whither are you going?

THIRD CITIZEN

Where do you dwell?

FOURTH CITIZEN

Are you a married man or a bachelor?

SECOND CITIZEN

Answer every man directly.

FIRST CITIZEN

Ay, and briefly.

FOURTH CITIZEN

Ay, and wisely.

THIRD CITIZEN

Ay, and truly, you were best.

CINNA THE POET

What is my name? Whither am I going? Where do I dwell? Am I a married man or a bachelor? Then, to answer every man directly and briefly, wisely and truly: wisely I say, I am a bachelor.

SECOND CITIZEN

That's as much as to say, they are fools that marry: you'll bear me a bang for that, I fear. Proceed; directly.

CINNA THE POET

Directly, I am going to Caesar's funeral.

FIRST CITIZEN

As a friend or an enemy?

CINNA THE POET

As a friend.

SECOND CITIZEN

That matter is answered directly.

FOURTH CITIZEN

For your dwelling—briefly.

CINNA THE POET

Briefly, I dwell by the Capitol.

THIRD CITIZEN

Your name, sir, truly.

CINNA THE POET

Truly, my name is Cinna.

FIRST CITIZEN

Tear him to pieces; he's a conspirator!

CINNA THE POET

I am Cinna the poet, I am Cinna the poet.

FOURTH CITIZEN

Tear him for his bad verses, tear him for his bad verses.

CINNA THE POET

I am not Cinna the conspirator.

FOURTH CITIZEN

It is no matter, his name's Cinna; pluck but his name out of his heart, and turn him going.

THIRD CITIZEN

Tear him, tear him! Come, brands ho! fire-brands! To Brutus', to Cassius'! Burn all! some to Decius' house, and some to Casca's; some to Ligarius'. Away, go!

Exeunt

Act 4

Scene I. A House in Rome.

ANTONY, OCTAVIUS, and LEPIDUS, seated at a table

ANTONY

These many, then, shall die; their names are prick'd.

OCTAVIUS

Your brother too must die. Consent you, Lepidus?

LEPIDUS

I do consent.

OCTAVIUS

Prick him down, Antony.

LEPIDUS

Upon condition Publius shall not live,

Who is your sister's son, Mark Antony.

ANTONY

He shall not live; look, with a spot I damn him.

But, Lepidus, go you to Caesar's house;

Fetch the will hither, and we shall determine
How to cut off some charge in legacies.

LEPIDUS

What, shall I find you here?

OCTAVIUS

Or here, or at the Capitol.

Exit LEPIDUS

ANTONY

This is a slight unmeritable man,
Meet to be sent on errands. Is it fit,
The three-fold world divided, he should stand
One of the three to share it?

OCTAVIUS

So you thought him;
And took his voice who should be prick'd to die,
In our black sentence and proscription.

ANTONY

Octavius, I have seen more days than you;
And though we lay these honours on this man,
To ease ourselves of divers slanderous loads,
He shall but bear them as the ass bears gold,
To groan and sweat under the business,
Either led or driven, as we point the way;
And having brought our treasure where we will,

Then take we down his load, and turn him off,
Like to the empty ass, to shake his ears,
And graze in commons.

OCTAVIUS

You may do your will;
But he's a tried and valiant soldier.

ANTONY

So is my horse, Octavius; and for that
I do appoint him store of provender:
It is a creature that I teach to fight,
To wind, to stop, to run directly on,
His corporal motion govern'd by my spirit.
And, in some taste, is Lepidus but so:
He must be taught and train'd and bid go forth;
A barren-spirited fellow; one that feeds
On abjects, orts and imitations,
Which, out of use and staled by other men,
Begin his fashion: do not talk of him,
But as a property. And now, Octavius,
Listen great things: Brutus and Cassius
Are levying powers: we must straight make head;
Therefore let our alliance be combined,
Our best friends made, our means stretch'd
And let us presently go sit in council,

How covert matters may be best disclosed,
And open perils surest answered.

OCTAVIUS

Let us do so; for we are at the stake,
And bay'd about with many enemies;
And some that smile have in their hearts, I fear,
Millions of mischiefs.

Exeunt

SCENE II. CAMP NEAR SARDIS. BEFORE BRUTUS'S TENT.

Drum. Enter BRUTUS, LUCILIUS, LUCIUS, and Soldiers; TITINIUS and PINDARUS meeting them

BRUTUS

Stand, ho!

LUCILIUS

Give the word, ho! and stand.

BRUTUS

What now, Lucilius? Is Cassius near?

LUCILIUS

He is at hand; and Pindarus is come
To do you salutation from his master.

BRUTUS

He greets me well. Your master, Pindarus,
In his own change, or by ill officers,
Hath given me some worthy cause to wish
Things done, undone: but, if he be at hand,
I shall be satisfied.

PINDARUS

I do not doubt
But that my noble master will appear
Such as he is, full of regard and honour.

BRUTUS

He is not doubted. A word, Lucilius;
How he received you, let me be resolved.

LUCILIUS

With courtesy and with respect enough;
But not with such familiar instances,
Nor with such free and friendly conference,
As he hath used of old.

BRUTUS

Thou hast described
A hot friend cooling: ever note, Lucilius,
When love begins to sicken and decay,
It useth an enforced ceremony.
There are no tricks in plain and simple faith;

But hollow men, like horses hot at hand,
Make gallant show and promise of their mettle;
But when they should endure the bloody spur,
They fall their crests, and, like deceitful jades,
Sink in the trial. Comes his army on?

LUCILIUS

They mean this night in Sardis to be quarter'd;
The greater part, the horse in general,
Are come with Cassius.

BRUTUS

Hark! he is arrived.

Low march within

March gently on to meet him.

Enter CASSIUS and his powers

CASSIUS

Stand, ho!

BRUTUS

Stand, ho! Speak the word along.

FIRST SOLDIER

Stand!

SECOND SOLDIER

Stand!

THIRD SOLDIER

Stand!

CASSIUS

Most noble brother, you have done me wrong.

BRUTUS

Judge me, you gods! wrong I mine enemies?
And, if not so, how should I wrong a brother?

CASSIUS

Brutus, this sober form of yours hides wrongs;
And when you do them—

BRUTUS

Cassius, be content;
Speak your griefs softly; I do know you well.
Before the eyes of both our armies here,
Which should perceive nothing but love from us,
Let us not wrangle. Bid them move away;
Then in my tent, Cassius, enlarge your griefs,
And I will give you audience.

CASSIUS

Pindarus,
Bid our commanders lead their charges off
A little from this ground.

BRUTUS

Lucilius, do you the like; and let no man
Come to our tent till we have done our
conference.

Let Lucius and Titinius guard our door.

Exeunt

SCENE III. BRUTUS'S TENT.

Enter BRUTUS and CASSIUS

CASSIUS

That you have wrong'd me doth appear in this:
You have condemn'd and noted Lucius Pella
For taking bribes here of the Sardians;
Wherein my letters, praying on his side,
Because I knew the man, were slighted off.

BRUTUS

You wronged yourself to write in such a case.

CASSIUS

In such a time as this it is not meet
That every nice offence should bear his comment.

BRUTUS

Let me tell you, Cassius, you yourself
Are much condemn'd to have an itching palm;
To sell and mart your offices for gold
To undeservers.

CASSIUS

I an itching palm!

You know that you are Brutus that speak this,

Or, by the gods, this speech were else your last.

BRUTUS

The name of Cassius honours this corruption,

And chastisement doth therefore hide his head.

CASSIUS

Chastisement!

BRUTUS

Remember March, the ides of March remember:

Did not great Julius bleed for justice' sake?

What villain touch'd his body, that did stab,

And not for justice? What, shall one of us

That struck the foremost man of all this world

But for supporting robbers, shall we now

Contaminate our fingers with base bribes,

And sell the mighty space of our large honours

For so much trash as may be grasped thus?

I had rather be a dog, and bay the moon,

Than such a Roman.

CASSIUS

Brutus, bay not me;

I'll not endure it: you forget yourself,

To hedge me in; I am a soldier, I,
Older in practise, abler than yourself
To make conditions.

BRUTUS

Go to; you are not, Cassius.

CASSIUS

I am.

BRUTUS

I say you are not.

CASSIUS

Urge me no more, I shall forget myself;
Have mind upon your health, tempt me no further.

BRUTUS

Away, slight man!

CASSIUS

Is't possible?

BRUTUS

Hear me, for I will speak.
Must I give way and room to your rash choler?
Shall I be frighted when a madman stares?

CASSIUS

O ye gods, ye gods! must I endure all this?

BRUTUS

All this! Ay, more! Fret till your proud heart break.

Go show your slaves how choleric you are,
And make your bondmen tremble. Must I budge?
Must I observe you? Must I stand and crouch
Under your testy humour? By the gods
You shall digest the venom of your spleen,
Though it do split you; for, from this day forth,
I'll use you for my mirth, yea, for my laughter,
When you are waspish.

CASSIUS

Is it come to this?

BRUTUS

You say you are a better soldier:
Let it appear so; make your vaunting true,
And it shall please me well: for mine own part,
I shall be glad to learn of noble men.

CASSIUS

You wrong me every way; you wrong me, Brutus;
I said, an elder soldier, not a better.
Did I say 'better'?

BRUTUS

If you did, I care not.

CASSIUS

When Caesar lived, he durst not thus have moved me.

BRUTUS

Peace, peace! You durst not so have tempted him.

CASSIUS

I durst not!

BRUTUS

No.

CASSIUS

What, durst not tempt him!

BRUTUS

For your life you durst not!

CASSIUS

Do not presume too much upon my love;
I may do that I shall be sorry for.

BRUTUS

You have done that you should be sorry for.
There is no terror, Cassius, in your threats,
For I am arm'd so strong in honesty
That they pass by me as the idle wind,
Which I respect not. I did send to you
For certain sums of gold, which you denied me;
For I can raise no money by vile means.
By heaven, I had rather coin my heart,
And drop my blood for drachmas, than to wring
From the hard hands of peasants their vile trash

By any indirection: I did send

To you for gold to pay my legions,

Which you denied me: was that done like Cassius?

Should I have answer'd Caius Cassius so?

When Marcus Brutus grows so covetous,

To lock such rascal counters from his friends,

Be ready, gods, with all your thunderbolts;

Dash him to pieces!

CASSIUS

I denied you not.

BRUTUS

You did.

CASSIUS

I did not. He was but a fool

That brought my answer back.

Brutus hath rived my heart.

A friend should bear his friend's infirmities,

But Brutus makes mine greater than they are.

BRUTUS

I do not, till you practise them on me.

CASSIUS

You love me not.

BRUTUS

I do not like your faults.

CASSIUS

A friendly eye could never see such faults.

BRUTUS

A flatterer's would not, though they do appear
As huge as high Olympus.

CASSIUS

Come, Antony, and young Octavius, come,
Revenge yourselves alone on Cassius,
For Cassius is aweary of the world;
Hated by one he loves; braved by his brother;
Check'd like a bondman; all his faults observed,
Set in a notebook, learn'd, and conn'd by rote,
To cast into my teeth. O, I could weep
My spirit from mine eyes! There is my dagger,
And here my naked breast; within, a heart
Dearer than Plutus' mine, richer than gold:
If that thou be'st a Roman, take it forth;
I, that denied thee gold, will give my heart:
Strike, as thou didst at Caesar; for, I know,
When thou didst hate him worst, thou lovedst him
better
Than ever thou lovedst Cassius.

BRUTUS

Sheathe your dagger:

Be angry when you will, it shall have scope;
Do what you will, dishonour shall be humour.
O Cassius, you are yoked with a lamb
That carries anger as the flint bears fire;
Who, much enforced, shows a hasty spark,
And straight is cold again.

CASSIUS

Hath Cassius lived
To be but mirth and laughter to his Brutus,
When grief, and blood ill-temper'd, vexeth him?

BRUTUS

When I spoke that, I was ill-temper'd too.

CASSIUS

Do you confess so much? Give me your hand.

BRUTUS

And my heart too.

CASSIUS

O Brutus!

BRUTUS

What's the matter?

CASSIUS

Have not you love enough to bear with me,
When that rash humour which my mother gave me
Makes me forgetful?

BRUTUS

Yes, Cassius; and, from henceforth,
When you are over-earnest with your Brutus,
He'll think your mother chides, and leave you so.

POET

[*Within*] Let me go in to see the generals;
There is some grudge between 'em, 'tis not meet
They be alone.

LUCILIUS

[*Within*] You shall not come to them.

POET

[*Within*] Nothing but death shall stay me.

Enter Poet, followed by LUCILIUS, TITINIUS, and LUCIUS

CASSIUS

How now! What's the matter?

POET

For shame, you generals! What do you mean?
Love, and be friends, as two such men should be;
For I have seen more years, I'm sure, than ye.

CASSIUS

Ha, ha! How vilely doth this cynic rhyme!

BRUTUS

Get you hence, sirrah; saucy fellow, hence!

CASSIUS

Bear with him, Brutus; 'tis his fashion.

BRUTUS

I'll know his humour, when he knows his time:
What should the wars do with these jigging fools?
Companion, hence!

CASSIUS

Away, away, be gone!

Exit Poet

BRUTUS

Lucilius and Titinius, bid the commanders
Prepare to lodge their companies to-night.

CASSIUS

And come yourselves, and bring Messala with you
Immediately to us.

Exeunt LUCILIUS and TITINIUS

BRUTUS

Lucius, a bowl of wine!

Exit LUCIUS

CASSIUS

I did not think you could have been so angry.

BRUTUS

O Cassius, I am sick of many griefs!

CASSIUS

Of your philosophy you make no use,

If you give place to accidental evils.

BRUTUS

No man bears sorrow better. Portia is dead.

CASSIUS

Ha! Portia?

BRUTUS

She is dead.

CASSIUS

How 'scaped I killing when I cross'd you so?

O insupportable and touching loss!

Upon what sickness?

BRUTUS

Impatient of my absence,

And grief that young Octavius with Mark Antony

Have made themselves so strong; for with her death

That tidings came—with this she fell distract,

And, her attendants absent, swallow'd fire.

CASSIUS

And died so?

BRUTUS

Even so.

CASSIUS

O ye immortal gods!

Re-enter LUCIUS, with wine and taper

BRUTUS

Speak no more of her. Give me a bowl of wine.

In this I bury all unkindness, Cassius.

CASSIUS

My heart is thirsty for that noble pledge.

Fill, Lucius, till the wine o'erswell the cup;

I cannot drink too much of Brutus' love.

BRUTUS

Come in, Titinius!

Exit LUCIUS

Re-enter TITINIUS,

with MESSALA

Welcome, good Messala!

Now sit we close about this taper here,

And call in question our necessities.

CASSIUS

Portia, art thou gone?

BRUTUS

No more, I pray you.

Messala, I have here received letters,

That young Octavius and Mark Antony

Come down upon us with a mighty power,
Bending their expedition toward Philippi.

MESSALA

Myself have letters of the selfsame tenor.

BRUTUS

With what addition?

MESSALA

That by proscription and bills of outlawry,
Octavius, Antony, and Lepidus,
Have put to death an hundred senators.

BRUTUS

Therein our letters do not well agree;
Mine speak of seventy senators that died
By their proscriptions, Cicero being one.

CASSIUS

Cicero one!

MESSALA

Cicero is dead,
And by that order of proscription.
Had you your letters from your wife, my lord?

BRUTUS

No, Messala.

MESSALA

Nor nothing in your letters writ of her?

BRUTUS

Nothing, Messala.

MESSALA

That, methinks, is strange.

BRUTUS

Why ask you? Hear you aught of her in yours?

MESSALA

No, my lord.

BRUTUS

Now, as you are a Roman, tell me true.

MESSALA

Then like a Roman bear the truth I tell:
For certain she is dead, and by strange manner.

BRUTUS

Why, farewell, Portia. We must die, Messala.
With meditating that she must die once,
I have the patience to endure it now.

MESSALA

Even so great men great losses should endure.

CASSIUS

I have as much of this in art as you,
But yet my nature could not bear it so.

BRUTUS

Well, to our work alive. What do you think

Of marching to Philippi presently?

CASSIUS

I do not think it good.

BRUTUS

Your reason?

CASSIUS

This it is:

'Tis better that the enemy seek us;

So shall he waste his means, weary his soldiers,

Doing himself offence; whilst we, lying still,

Are full of rest, defense, and nimbleness.

BRUTUS

Good reasons must, of force, give place to better.

The people 'twixt Philippi and this ground

Do stand but in a forced affection;

For they have grudged us contribution:

The enemy, marching along by them,

By them shall make a fuller number up,

Come on refresh'd, new-added, and encouraged;

From which advantage shall we cut him off,

If at Philippi we do face him there,

These people at our back.

CASSIUS

Hear me, good brother.

BRUTUS

Under your pardon. You must note beside,
That we have tried the utmost of our friends,
Our legions are brim-full, our cause is ripe:
The enemy increaseth every day;
We, at the height, are ready to decline.
There is a tide in the affairs of men,
Which, taken at the flood, leads on to fortune;
Omitted, all the voyage of their life
Is bound in shallows and in miseries.
On such a full sea are we now afloat;
And we must take the current when it serves,
Or lose our ventures.

CASSIUS

Then, with your will, go on;
We'll along ourselves, and meet them at Philippi.

BRUTUS

The deep of night is crept upon our talk,
And nature must obey necessity;
Which we will niggard with a little rest.
There is no more to say?

CASSIUS

No more. Good night:
Early to-morrow will we rise, and hence.

BRUTUS

Lucius!

Enter LUCIUS

My gown.

Exit LUCIUS

Farewell, good Messala.
Good night, Titinius. Noble, noble Cassius,
Good night, and good repose!

CASSIUS

O my dear brother,
This was an ill beginning of the night!
Never come such division 'tween our souls!
Let it not, Brutus.

BRUTUS

Everything is well.

CASSIUS

Good night, my lord.

BRUTUS

Good night, good brother.

TITINIUS MESSALA

Good night, Lord Brutus.

BRUTUS

Farewell, every one.

Exeunt all but BRUTUS

Re-enter LUCIUS, with the gown

Give me the gown. Where is thy instrument?

LUCIUS

Here in the tent.

BRUTUS

What, thou speak'st drowsily?

Poor knave, I blame thee not; thou art o'erwatch'd.

Call Claudius and some other of my men:

I'll have them sleep on cushions in my tent.

LUCIUS

Varro and Claudius!

Enter VARRO and CLAUDIUS

VARRO

Calls my lord?

BRUTUS

I pray you, sirs, lie in my tent and sleep;

It may be I shall raise you by and by

On business to my brother Cassius.

VARRO

So please you, we will stand and watch your pleasure.

BRUTUS

I will not have it so. Lie down, good sirs;

It may be I shall otherwise bethink me.
Look, Lucius, here's the book I sought for so;
I put it in the pocket of my gown.

VARRO and CLAUDIUS lie down

LUCIUS

I was sure your lordship did not give it me.

BRUTUS

Bear with me, good boy, I am much forgetful.
Canst thou hold up thy heavy eyes awhile,
And touch thy instrument a strain or two?

LUCIUS

Ay, my lord, an't please you.

BRUTUS

It does, my boy.
I trouble thee too much, but thou art willing.

LUCIUS

It is my duty, sir.

BRUTUS

I should not urge thy duty past thy might;
I know young bloods look for a time of rest.

LUCIUS

I have slept, my lord, already.

BRUTUS

It was well done; and thou shalt sleep again;

I will not hold thee long: if I do live,
I will be good to thee.

Music, and a song

This is a sleepy tune. O murderous slumber!
Lay'st thou thy leaden mace upon my boy,
That plays thee music? Gentle knave, good night;
I will not do thee so much wrong to wake thee:
If thou dost nod, thou break'st thy instrument;
I'll take it from thee; and, good boy, good night.
Let me see, let me see; is not the leaf turn'd down
Where I left reading? Here it is, I think.

Enter the Ghost of CAESAR

How ill this taper burns! Ha! who comes here?
I think it is the weakness of mine eyes
That shapes this monstrous apparition.
It comes upon me. Art thou anything?
Art thou some god, some angel, or some devil,
That makest my blood cold and my hair to stare?
Speak to me what thou art.

GHOST

Thy evil spirit, Brutus.

BRUTUS

Why comest thou?

GHOST

To tell thee thou shalt see me at Philippi.

BRUTUS

Well; then I shall see thee again?

GHOST

Ay, at Philippi.

BRUTUS

Why, I will see thee at Philippi, then.

Exit Ghost

Now I have taken heart thou vanishest:

Ill spirit, I would hold more talk with thee.

Boy, Lucius! Varro! Claudius! Sirs, awake!

Claudius!

LUCIUS

The strings, my lord, are false.

BRUTUS

He thinks he still is at his instrument.

Lucius, awake!

LUCIUS

My lord!

BRUTUS

Didst thou dream, Lucius, that thou so criedst out?

LUCIUS

My lord, I do not know that I did cry.

BRUTUS

Yes, that thou didst. Didst thou see anything?

LUCIUS

Nothing, my lord.

BRUTUS

Sleep again, Lucius. Sirrah Claudius!

To VARRO

Fellow thou, awake!

VARRO

My lord?

CLAUDIUS

My lord?

BRUTUS

Why did you so cry out, sirs, in your sleep?

VARRO CLAUDIUS

Did we, my lord?

BRUTUS

Ay: saw you anything?

VARRO

No, my lord, I saw nothing.

CLAUDIUS

Nor I, my lord.

BRUTUS

Go and commend me to my brother Cassius;

Bid him set on his powers betimes before,

And we will follow.

VARRO CLAUDIUS

It shall be done, my lord.

Exeunt

Act 5

SCENE I. THE PLAINS OF PHILIPPI.

Enter OCTAVIUS, ANTONY, and their army

OCTAVIUS

Now, Antony, our hopes are answered:
You said the enemy would not come down,
But keep the hills and upper regions;
It proves not so: their battles are at hand;
They mean to warn us at Philippi here,
Answering before we do demand of them.

ANTONY

Tut, I am in their bosoms, and I know
Wherefore they do it: they could be content
To visit other places; and come down
With fearful bravery, thinking by this face
To fasten in our thoughts that they have courage;
But 'tis not so.

Enter a Messenger

MESSENGER

Prepare you, generals:
The enemy comes on in gallant show;
Their bloody sign of battle is hung out,
And something to be done immediately.

ANTONY

Octavius, lead your battle softly on,
Upon the left hand of the even field.

OCTAVIUS

Upon the right hand I; keep thou the left.

ANTONY

Why do you cross me in this exigent?

OCTAVIUS

I do not cross you; but I will do so.

March

Drum. Enter BRUTUS, CASSIUS, and their Army; LUCILIUS, TITINIUS, MESSALA, and others

BRUTUS

They stand, and would have parley.

CASSIUS

Stand fast, Titinius: we must out and talk.

OCTAVIUS

Mark Antony, shall we give sign of battle?

ANTONY

No, Caesar, we will answer on their charge.

Make forth; the generals would have some words.

OCTAVIUS

Stir not until the signal.

BRUTUS

Words before blows. Is it so, countrymen?

OCTAVIUS

Not that we love words better, as you do.

BRUTUS

Good words are better than bad strokes,

Octavius.

ANTONY

In your bad strokes, Brutus, you give good

words:

Witness the hole you made in Caesar's heart,

Crying 'Long live! Hail, Caesar!'

CASSIUS

Antony,

The posture of your blows are yet unknown;

But for your words, they rob the Hybla bees,

And leave them honeyless.

ANTONY

Not stingless too.

BRUTUS

O, yes, and soundless too;
For you have stol'n their buzzing, Antony,
And very wisely threat before you sting.

ANTONY

Villains, you did not so, when your vile daggers
Hack'd one another in the sides of Caesar:
You show'd your teeth like apes, and fawn'd like hounds,
And bow'd like bondmen, kissing Caesar's feet;
Whilst damned Casca, like a cur, behind
Struck Caesar on the neck. O you flatterers!

CASSIUS

Flatterers! Now, Brutus, thank yourself:
This tongue had not offended so to-day,
If Cassius might have ruled.

OCTAVIUS

Come, come, the cause: if arguing make us sweat,
The proof of it will turn to redder drops. Look;
I draw a sword against conspirators;
When think you that the sword goes up again?
Never, till Caesar's three and thirty wounds
Be well avenged; or till another Caesar
Have added slaughter to the sword of traitors.

BRUTUS

Caesar, thou canst not die by traitors' hands,
Unless thou bring'st them with thee.

OCTAVIUS

So I hope;
I was not born to die on Brutus' sword.

BRUTUS

O, if thou wert the noblest of thy strain,
Young man, thou couldst not die more honourable.

CASSIUS

A peevish schoolboy, worthless of such honour,
Join'd with a masker and a reveller!

ANTONY

Old Cassius still!

OCTAVIUS

Come, Antony, away!
Defiance, traitors, hurl we in your teeth:
If you dare fight to-day, come to the field;
If not, when you have stomachs.

Exeunt OCTAVIUS, ANTONY, and their army

CASSIUS

Why, now, blow wind, swell billow and swim bark!
The storm is up, and all is on the hazard.

BRUTUS

Ho, Lucilius! hark, a word with you.

LUCILIUS

[*Standing forth*] My lord?

BRUTUS and LUCILIUS converse apart

CASSIUS

Messala!

MESSALA

[*Standing forth*] What says my general?

CASSIUS

Messala,
This is my birth-day; as this very day
Was Cassius born. Give me thy hand, Messala.
Be thou my witness that against my will,
As Pompey was, am I compell'd to set
Upon one battle all our liberties.
You know that I held Epicurus strong
And his opinion: now I change my mind,
And partly credit things that do presage.
Coming from Sardis, on our former ensign
Two mighty eagles fell, and there they perch'd,
Gorging and feeding from our soldiers' hands;
Who to Philippi here consorted us:
This morning are they fled away and gone;

And in their steads do ravens, crows and kites,
Fly o'er our heads and downward look on us,
As we were sickly prey: their shadows seem
A canopy most fatal, under which
Our army lies, ready to give up the ghost.

MESSALA

Believe not so.

CASSIUS

I but believe it partly;
For I am fresh of spirit and resolved
To meet all perils very constantly.

BRUTUS

Even so, Lucilius.

CASSIUS

Now, most noble Brutus,
The gods to-day stand friendly, that we may,
Lovers in peace, lead on our days to age!
But since the affairs of men rest still incertain,
Let's reason with the worst that may befall.
If we do lose this battle, then is this
The very last time we shall speak together.
What are you then determined to do?

BRUTUS

Even by the rule of that philosophy

By which I did blame Cato for the death
Which he did give himself, I know not how,
But I do find it cowardly and vile,
For fear of what might fall, so to prevent
The time of life—arming myself with patience
To stay the providence of some high powers
That govern us below.

CASSIUS

Then, if we lose this battle,
You are contented to be led in triumph
Thorough the streets of Rome?

BRUTUS

No, Cassius, no: think not, thou noble Roman,
That ever Brutus will go bound to Rome;
He bears too great a mind. But this same day
Must end that work the ides of March begun;
And whether we shall meet again I know not.
Therefore our everlasting farewell take:
For ever, and for ever, farewell, Cassius!
If we do meet again, why, we shall smile;
If not, why then, this parting was well made.

CASSIUS

For ever, and for ever, farewell, Brutus!
If we do meet again, we'll smile indeed;

If not, 'tis true this parting was well made.

BRUTUS

Why, then, lead on. O, that a man might know
The end of this day's business ere it come!
But it sufficeth that the day will end,
And then the end is known. Come, ho! away!

Exeunt

SCENE II. THE SAME. THE FIELD OF BATTLE.

Alarum. Enter BRUTUS and MESSALA

BRUTUS

Ride, ride, Messala, ride, and give these bills
Unto the legions on the other side.

Loud alarum

Let them set on at once; for I perceive
But cold demeanor in Octavius' wing,
And sudden push gives them the overthrow.
Ride, ride, Messala: let them all come down.

Exeunt

Scene III. Another Part of the Field.

Alarums. Enter CASSIUS and TITINIUS

CASSIUS

O, look, Titinius, look, the villains fly!
Myself have to mine own turn'd enemy.
This ensign here of mine was turning back;
I slew the coward, and did take it from him.

TITINIUS

O Cassius, Brutus gave the word too early;
Who, having some advantage on Octavius,
Took it too eagerly: his soldiers fell to spoil,
Whilst we by Antony are all enclosed.

Enter PINDARUS

PINDARUS

Fly further off, my lord, fly further off;
Mark Antony is in your tents, my lord
Fly, therefore, noble Cassius, fly far off.

CASSIUS

This hill is far enough. Look, look, Titinius;
Are those my tents where I perceive the fire?

TITINIUS

They are, my lord.

CASSIUS

Titinius, if thou lovest me,
Mount thou my horse, and hide thy spurs in him,
Till he have brought thee up to yonder troops,
And here again; that I may rest assured
Whether yond troops are friend or enemy.

TITINIUS

I will be here again, even with a thought.

Exit

CASSIUS

Go, Pindarus, get higher on that hill;
My sight was ever thick; regard Titinius,
And tell me what thou notest about the field.

PINDARUS ascends the hill

This day I breathed first: time is come round,
And where I did begin, there shall I end;
My life is run his compass. Sirrah, what news?

PINDARUS

[*Above*] O my lord!

CASSIUS

What news?

PINDARUS

[*Above*] Titinius is enclosed round about
With horsemen, that make to him on the spur;

Yet he spurs on. Now they are almost on him.
Now, Titinius! Now some light. O, he lights too.
He's ta'en.

Shout

And, hark! They shout for joy.

CASSIUS

Come down; behold no more.
O, coward that I am, to live so long,
To see my best friend ta'en before my face!

PINDARUS descends

Come hither, sirrah:
In Parthia did I take thee prisoner;
And then I swore thee, saving of thy life,
That whatsoever I did bid thee do,
Thou shouldst attempt it. Come now, keep thine oath;
Now be a freeman: and with this good sword,
That ran through Caesar's bowels, search this bosom.
Stand not to answer: here, take thou the hilts;
And, when my face is cover'd, as 'tis now,
Guide thou the sword.

PINDARUS stabs him

Caesar, thou art revenged,

Even with the sword that kill'd thee.

Dies

PINDARUS

So, I am free; yet would not so have been,
Durst I have done my will. O Cassius,
Far from this country Pindarus shall run,
Where never Roman shall take note of him.

Exit

Re-enter TITINIUS with MESSALA

MESSALA

It is but change, Titinius; for Octavius
Is overthrown by noble Brutus' power,
As Cassius' legions are by Antony.

TITINIUS

These tidings will well comfort Cassius.

MESSALA

Where did you leave him?

TITINIUS

All disconsolate,
With Pindarus his bondman, on this hill.

MESSALA

Is not that he t hat lies upon the ground?

TITINIUS

He lies not like the living. O my heart!

MESSALA

Is not that he?

TITINIUS

No, this was he, Messala,
But Cassius is no more. O setting sun,
As in thy red rays thou dost sink to-night,
So in his red blood Cassius' day is set;
The sun of Rome is set! Our day is gone;
Clouds, dews, and dangers come; our deeds are done!
Mistrust of my success hath done this deed.

MESSALA

Mistrust of good success hath done this deed.
O hateful error, melancholy's child,
Why dost thou show to the apt thoughts of men
The things that are not? O error, soon conceived,
Thou never comest unto a happy birth,
But kill'st the mother that engender'd thee!

TITINIUS

What, Pindarus! Where art thou, Pindarus?

MESSALA

Seek him, Titinius, whilst I go to meet
The noble Brutus, thrusting this report
Into his ears; I may say, thrusting it;

For piercing steel and darts envenomed
Shall be as welcome to the ears of Brutus
As tidings of this sight.

TITINIUS

Hie you, Messala,
And I will seek for Pindarus the while.

Exit MESSALA

Why didst thou send me forth, brave Cassius?
Did I not meet thy friends? and did not they
Put on my brows this wreath of victory,
And bid me give it thee? Didst thou not hear their shouts?
Alas, thou hast misconstrued every thing!
But, hold thee, take this garland on thy brow;
Thy Brutus bid me give it thee, and I
Will do his bidding. Brutus, come apace,
And see how I regarded Caius Cassius.
By your leave, gods—this is a Roman's part
Come, Cassius' sword, and find Titinius' heart.

Kills himself

Alarum. Re-enter MESSALA, with BRUTUS, CATO, STRATO, VOLUMNIUS, and LUCILIUS

BRUTUS

Where, where, Messala, doth his body lie?

MESSALA

Lo, yonder, and Titinius mourning it.

BRUTUS

Titinius' face is upward.

CATO

He is slain.

BRUTUS

O Julius Caesar, thou art mighty yet!
Thy spirit walks abroad and turns our swords
In our own proper entrails.

Low alarums

CATO

Brave Titinius!
Look, whether he have not crown'd dead Cassius!

BRUTUS

Are yet two Romans living such as these?
The last of all the Romans, fare thee well!
It is impossible that ever Rome
Should breed thy fellow. Friends, I owe more tears
To this dead man than you shall see me pay.
I shall find time, Cassius, I shall find time.
Come, therefore, and to Thasos send his body:
His funerals shall not be in our camp,
Lest it discomfort us. Lucilius, come;

And come, young Cato; let us to the field.

Labeo and Flavius, set our battles on:

'Tis three o'clock; and, Romans, yet ere night

We shall try fortune in a second fight.

Exeunt

SCENE IV. ANOTHER PART OF THE FIELD.

Alarum. Enter fighting, Soldiers of both armies; then BRUTUS, CATO, LUCILIUS, and others

BRUTUS

Yet, countrymen, O, yet hold up your heads!

CATO

What bastard doth not? Who will go with me?

I will proclaim my name about the field:

I am the son of Marcus Cato, ho!

A foe to tyrants, and my country's friend;

I am the son of Marcus Cato, ho!

BRUTUS

And I am Brutus, Marcus Brutus, I;

Brutus, my country's friend; know me for Brutus!

Exit

LUCILIUS

O young and noble Cato, art thou down?

Why, now thou diest as bravely as Titinius;

And mayst be honour'd, being Cato's son.

FIRST SOLDIER

Yield, or thou diest.

LUCILIUS

Only I yield to die.

There is so much that thou wilt kill me straight.

Offering money

Kill Brutus, and be honour'd in his death.

FIRST SOLDIER

We must not. A noble prisoner!

SECOND SOLDIER

Room, ho! Tell Antony, Brutus is ta'en.

FIRST SOLDIER

I'll tell the news. Here comes the general.

Enter ANTONY

Brutus is ta'en, Brutus is ta'en, my lord.

ANTONY

Where is he?

LUCILIUS

Safe, Antony; Brutus is safe enough.

I dare assure thee that no enemy

Shall ever take alive the noble Brutus.

The gods defend him from so great a shame!

When you do find him, or alive or dead,
He will be found like Brutus, like himself.

ANTONY

This is not Brutus, friend; but, I assure you,
A prize no less in worth: keep this man safe;
Give him all kindness: I had rather have
Such men my friends than enemies. Go on,
And see whether Brutus be alive or dead;
And bring us word unto Octavius' tent
How every thing is chanced.

Exeunt

Scene V. Another Part of The Field.

Enter BRUTUS, DARDANIUS, CLITUS, STRATO, and VOLUMNIUS

BRUTUS

Come, poor remains of friends, rest on this rock.

CLITUS

Statilius show'd the torchlight, but, my lord,
He came not back: he is or ta'en or slain.

BRUTUS

Sit thee down, Clitus: slaying is the word;
It is a deed in fashion. Hark thee, Clitus.

Whispers

CLITUS

What, I, my lord? No, not for all the world.

BRUTUS

Peace then! no words.

CLITUS

I'll rather kill myself.

BRUTUS

Hark thee, Dardanius!

Whispers

DARDANIUS

Shall I do such a deed?

CLITUS

O Dardanius!

DARDANIUS

O Clitus!

CLITUS

What ill request did Brutus make to thee?

DARDANIUS

To kill him, Clitus. Look, he meditates.

CLITUS

Now is that noble vessel full of grief,
That it runs over even at his eyes.

BRUTUS

Come hither, good Volumnius; list a word.

VOLUMNIUS

What says my lord?

BRUTUS

Why, this, Volumnius:
The ghost of Caesar hath appear'd to me
Two several times by night; at Sardis once,
And, this last night, here in Philippi fields:
I know my hour is come.

VOLUMNIUS

Not so, my lord.

BRUTUS

Nay, I am sure it is, Volumnius.
Thou seest the world, Volumnius, how it goes;
Our enemies have beat us to the pit:

Low alarums

It is more worthy to leap in ourselves,
Than tarry till they push us. Good Volumnius,
Thou know'st that we two went to school together:
Even for that our love of old, I prithee,
Hold thou my sword-hilts, whilst I run on it.

VOLUMNIUS

That's not an office for a friend, my lord.

Alarum still

CLITUS

Fly, fly, my lord; there is no tarrying here.

BRUTUS

Farewell to you; and you; and you, Volumnius.
Strato, thou hast been all this while asleep;
Farewell to thee too, Strato. Countrymen,
My heart doth joy that yet in all my life
I found no man but he was true to me.
I shall have glory by this losing day
More than Octavius and Mark Antony
By this vile conquest shall attain unto.
So fare you well at once; for Brutus' tongue
Hath almost ended his life's history:
Night hangs upon mine eyes; my bones would rest,
That have but labour'd to attain this hour.

Alarum. Cry within, 'Fly, fly, fly!'

CLITUS

Fly, my lord, fly.

BRUTUS

Hence! I will follow.

Exeunt CLITUS, DARDANIUS, and VOLUMNIUS

I prithee, Strato, stay thou by thy lord:

Thou art a fellow of a good respect;
Thy life hath had some smatch of honour in it.
Hold then my sword, and turn away thy face,
While I do run upon it. Wilt thou, Strato?

STRATO

Give me your hand first. Fare you well, my lord.

BRUTUS

Farewell, good Strato.

Runs on his sword

Caesar, now be still:
I kill'd not thee with half so good a will.

Dies

Alarum. Retreat. Enter OCTAVIUS, ANTONY, MESSALA, LUCILIUS, and the army

OCTAVIUS

What man is that?

MESSALA

My master's man. Strato, where is thy master?

STRATO

Free from the bondage you are in, Messala:
The conquerors can but make a fire of him;
For Brutus only overcame himself,
And no man else hath honour by his death.

LUCILIUS

So Brutus should be found. I thank thee, Brutus,

That thou hast proved Lucilius' saying true.

OCTAVIUS

All that served Brutus, I will entertain them.

Fellow, wilt thou bestow thy time with me?

STRATO

Ay, if Messala will prefer me to you.

OCTAVIUS

Do so, good Messala.

MESSALA

How died my master, Strato?

STRATO

I held the sword, and he did run on it.

MESSALA

Octavius, then take him to follow thee,

That did the latest service to my master.

ANTONY

This was the noblest Roman of them all.

All the conspirators save only he

Did that they did in envy of great Caesar;

He only, in a general honest thought

And common good to all, made one of them.

His life was gentle, and the elements

So mix'd in him that Nature might stand up
And say to all the world 'This was a man!'

OCTAVIUS

According to his virtue let us use him,
With all respect and rites of burial.
Within my tent his bones to-night shall lie,
Most like a soldier, order'd honourably.
So call the field to rest; and let's away,
To part the glories of this happy day.

Exeunt